The Fire Stallion

Stacy Gregg

HarperCollins *Children's Books*

First published in Great Britain by
HarperCollins *Children's Books* in 2018
Published in this edition in 2019
HarperCollins *Children's Books* is a division of HarperCollins*Publishers* Ltd,
HarperCollins Publishers
1 London Bridge Street
London SE1 9GF

The HarperCollins website address is:
www.harpercollins.co.uk
1

ISBN 978-0-00-826142-9

Stacy Gregg asserts the moral right to be identified as the author of the work.
A CIP catalogue record for this title is available from the British Library.

Typeset by Palimpsest Book Production Limited, Falkirk, Stirlingshire
Printed and bound in England by CPI Group (UK) Ltd, Croydon CR0 4YY

MIX
Paper from
responsible sources
FSC
www.fsc.org
FSC™ C007454

This book is produced from independently certified FSC™ paper
to ensure responsible forest management.

Find out more about HarperCollins and the environment at
www.harpercollins.co.uk/green

The Fire
Stallion

For Nicky Pellegrino
and the Sea Breeze Café

Chapter 1

Eternal Dawn

When I was little, I was terrified of the dark. I was totally convinced that night-time brought the monsters to life.

I never thought that one day I would miss it. That I would be here now, lying in bed wide awake at midnight, longing for the peaceful inky blackness of a true night sky.

When I push apart the blackout curtains in our log cabin it's as bright as day outside. Lilac clouds sweep in drifts across the sky, their edges rimmed with fiery shades of pink. At the horizon the sky deepens into blood red until the point where it strikes the sea and becomes molten gold.

Nobody mentioned the constant daylight to me

before we arrived in Iceland. Mum had told me it was going to be freezing here, even though it's the middle of summer, but she never said that in summer there's virtually no night. It's because we're so close to the North Pole. The sun pretty much never sets.

You would think that continual daytime would be cool – like staying up as late as you want. But it's not like that. Eventually, you want to sleep whatever, and then you find that you can't because, even with the blackout curtains, those rays find a way of creeping in. Just knowing that the sun is blazing outside while you're in bed trying to sleep is enough to keep you wide awake.

No wonder this place is messing with my head. Ever since that night with the fire ritual, I swear that I'm not always me any more. I shift back and forth, my shape becoming one and the same as hers. If I focus hard now, I can hear her voice. More than that, I can feel her thoughts and instincts. They're mingled with mine. Brunhilda's Viking blood is coursing through my veins. I'm a thousand years old and thirteen all at the same time.

Yesterday, as I walked across the fields towards the horses with Anders I saw this patch of brilliant red berries growing right there on the moss beside the track. Without thinking, I picked some and put them straight in my mouth. Anders was horrified.

"Are you crazy? They could be poisonous!"

I laughed. "They're delicious," I insisted, holding them out to him. "Try some!"

I would have been in big trouble if Katherine had caught me. Feeding potentially poisonous wild berries to her lead actor? She would have hit the roof. I'm not even a proper crew member on this movie, I'm only here because of Mum.

Anders hesitated for longer than I expected. "How do you know, Hilly? If they're poisonous, they could kill us," he said.

"I've got no intention of dying," I replied, smiling. My hand was still outstretched, daring him to take them.

"Nobody intends to die," Anders said, plucking the entire handful from my palm and then munching them down.

"Yummy," he agreed.

I double-checked the berries on the internet when I

was back at the cabin later that day. Lingonberries, it said. They turn scarlet when ripe for the picking. Perfectly safe. A staple of the ancient Icelandic diet. But then I had known that when I had picked them. It's because of Brunhilda. I know everything that she knows. All about the natural world around me here. Like I can tell you which are the tastiest of the mosses and lichens growing on the volcanic rocks. I'm an expert too on gathering seaweed, picking through the salty strands washed up on the shoreline, divining which kinds are suited for eating raw and which would be better for stewing in the cooking pot. The other day, walking along the beach, I found a dead Greenland shark that had washed up in the storm and, without even acknowledging what I was doing, I found myself digging a hole in the pebbles at the top of the tideline, where I knew it would stay dry, and burying the body. I dug the hole shallow, but deep enough so that the heavy stones I piled up on top will press down and squeeze the shark, making the deadly toxins leach out as it rots. It will need about a month like that before I can go back and dig it up again and eat it. By then its noxious juices will have disappeared completely and the meat will be safe to consume.

I mean, come on! How did I know that? Since when is the process of fermenting a Greenland shark something a kid from New Zealand knows how to do?

My connection to Iceland becomes more powerful every day. There's a magnetic pull that anchors me here. I can hear the land humming with energy, can feel its volcanic vibrations beneath my feet and in the air.

I don't tell Mum any of this stuff. She's fed up with what she calls all the "mystical mumbo jumbo" that's been happening to me since we arrived. Mum's very practical and hasn't got much patience for hippy-drippy nonsense. As the head of the costume design team, she spends all day dealing with highly strung actors and actresses banging on about their spirituality, and it has made her intolerant.

That's why Mum can't stand Gudrun. I know a lot of the crew totally agree with Mum and think that the cultural consultant is either a schemer or simply nuts. Behind her back they call her "the Icelandic witch" because she swans about in these floaty dresses, burning bunches of sage and chanting Norse poetry.

Nobody can do anything about Gudrun, though, because Katherine, the film director, is the one who brought her along. Gudrun's a professor of Icelandic saga, and knows everything about the real-life Brunhilda of the film.

"'Cultural consultant' is a fancy term for getting in the way and holding up the rest of us who have real jobs to do," Mum complained after that first day of filming, when Gudrun made everyone run late by insisting that the whole crew formed a circle round her while she chanted and "blessed" the set.

Mum says that Gudrun is crazy, or just very good at acting crazy to keep her job. Either way, Mum really doesn't like me hanging out with her. But she's wrong about Gudrun. I know her rituals are annoying, but she's not faking it. Gudrun is one hundred per cent serious. She truly believes in everything she's doing.

I remember when we got off the plane at Keflavik airport and Gudrun sidled up to me. She put her pale arm round my shoulder, pulling me close to her so that no one else could listen when she whispered, "Hilly, do you hear the land crying out to you? Iceland knows that the Norse heir to the throne has returned to her. You are home. You are home."

And it's true – I am home. I belong here. Or perhaps that's the sleep deprivation talking. It's 2 a.m. and I still can't sleep. I get out of bed and pull on jeans and Ugg boots, along with my thickest woollen pullover and a North Face puffer jacket. Then I head out of the cabin and down the woodland path that takes me between the crew's cabins, all the way to the fields beyond.

It's midsummer and yet it's so cold my breath makes puffs of steam in the air as I walk. I have to shove my hands deep in my pockets to stop my fingers from going numb.

At the edge of the cabins there's a stile I clamber over and I keep on going, the gravel of the path crunching lightly beneath my feet. The moss on either side of the path is a washed-out sage green. If you step on it, your foot leaves an imprint then slowly springs back up. Halfway to the fields the moss clears and now the soil turns black. There's steam rising up from hot pools that are deep enough to climb into at the end of a hard day's filming.

Beyond the black steaming rocks, more moss grows, and then rust-coloured heather and tussock grass form little islands in among the marshlands. This is where Mjölnir lives.

When Mjölnir arrived, the crew all had trouble

pronouncing his name – for the record you say it "Meel-nir". Anyway, no one could get it right so we called him Hammer, because that's what Mjölnir is: he's the hammer of the gods – the weapon that once belonged to the mighty Thor.

At the edge of the marshlands I stand with my hands cupped at my mouth and call his name.

"Hammer! Hammer!"

Nothing.

He could be sleeping, I guess. He doesn't have the same sort of insomnia as I have. He was born here and he thinks it's perfectly normal to sleep in daylight.

"Hammer!" I try again and this time, in response to my call, a clarion cry thunders through the air, echoing across the fields.

And then I see him. He flits between the trees of the woods like a black shadow. His mane is flying wild, like brilliant scarlet silk ribbons in the wind, and his tail flashes behind him as if it's on fire.

Gudrun says she threw the runes and asked the gods to bring her the perfect horse. She believes that all of this was fated to happen – me and her and Hammer too.

Looking back, she was preparing Hammer to be with

me right from the start, just as she was readying me for the rituals of Jonsmessa, preparing me to make the Cross-Over when the time came. I only wish I had known that back then, but I guess if Gudrun had told me the truth about Jonsmessa I would have thought she was crazy, too.

You're going to think I'm mad myself, unless I backtrack and start at the beginning… unless I tell you how I ended up in this remote land of volcanoes and ice at the furthest end of the world.

It's no coincidence that I'm here. Gudrun is right about that. She read in the runes that I would come and I have. I am here in Iceland to do what needs to be done for the saga. To make things right at last, not for me but for *her*. I will fight this battle to redeem Brunhilda and bring glory to the one true queen. Her saga has been told before, but this time there's a twist. This time we're in it together.

CHAPTER 2

Horses in the Woods

L ooking back, I can see that Gudrun had been preparing me before we'd even got to Iceland. It began the moment I met her, that first night in London.

This was the first time that Mum had taken me on one of her film jobs and I was nervous about tagging along to dinner that night. Katherine Kara, the director of *Brunhilda*, had decided to throw a get-together for the crew at a Japanese restaurant in Soho before we departed for Reykjavik.

Mum and I had only just arrived that morning on the long-haul flight from New Zealand. I was so jetlagged my brain was swimming and I could barely talk. "We can go back to the hotel and get room service instead if you're tired?" Mum said, looking worried.

"I'll be fine," I promised. I knew that Mum felt unprofessional having her daughter along. It had never been the plan to bring me and it would never have happened if things hadn't turned out like they did with Piper.

It had been the start of the eventing season. I'd been doing loads of fitness work on Piper, riding her on the beach each day, doing timed gallops along stretches of hard sand and then cooling her legs by walking her home in the salt water. We'd finished the season at the top of the one-metre class rankings at the end of last year and were about to step up to the big league. Taking on the Open class fences at a metre ten was like going pro, but we were ready for it. Nothing was going to stop us. Until it did.

It's an odd thing because I don't usually check on Piper at night, but that evening something made me go to her paddock. As soon as I saw her lying down like that, I knew. She was in this weird position, her neck craned uncomfortably, and she was sniffing at her belly, as though she was about to have a foal, except she couldn't be – she wasn't pregnant. I climbed over the gate and ran across to her, and when I reached her I could hear her making these groans, and then she nickered to me with this pitiful cry as if she was saying, "Oh, thank goodness you're here – I'm in such pain!"

I pulled at her neck rug and got her to stand up, but almost straight away she dropped back to her knees and was lying down again. Then she kicked out at her stomach, really hard, so that she actually struck it with her right hind leg and then she collapsed back to the ground with an agonised groan.

"Piper!" I dropped to the ground, undoing her rug, seeing how soaked in sweat she was beneath it. I needed help.

"I'll be back," I promised her.

I remember running to the house, stumbling in the dark, feeling like I was going to throw up, and then I couldn't find Mum or Dad anywhere and I was yelling for them and finally Mum came into the kitchen and found me sobbing.

"Hilly? What's going on?"

"It's Piper!" I couldn't breathe to get the words out. "She's got colic."

Mum looked at me, her face ashen. "You go back to her," she said. "I'll call the vet."

Piper was still on the ground when I got to her again. It took me, Mum and Dad to get her up on her feet. Then, for the next hour and a half while we waited for the vet to come, I had to keep her up. A horse with colic doesn't realise what's wrong. All they know is that their gut hurts, and so they can injure themselves really badly by trying to kick their own stomachs and you have to keep them walking to stop them from harming themselves. And so I walked her, in circles, around and around the yard, waiting for the vet to arrive. When it was almost midnight Mum had offered to take a turn, but I said no. Piper was my horse and she trusted me, I had to stay with her. Besides, I was so sick with fear I needed to keep doing something.

I had been so relieved when I'd seen the headlights of the vet's truck snaking their way down the bush road that led to our farm. It turned straight towards the stables and when she got out of the truck she immediately began grabbing vials and needles out of her supply kit, gathering everything she needed before she ran to join us.

"Sorry it's taken me so long," she said. "I was

delivering a foal on the other side of the gorge and there are no other vets on call tonight."

She took out her stethoscope and began to listen to Piper's heartbeat. I stayed silent, letting her concentrate.

"How long has she been like this?" she asked.

"I don't know," I said. "I found her at around seven thirty, so at least since then."

The vet filled a syringe and injected Piper in the neck.

"What's that?" Mum asked.

"Muscle relaxant," she said. "You were right. It's colic. Hopefully, if the relaxant works, then the contractions should subside."

"And if it doesn't work?" I asked.

The vet didn't look at me and she didn't answer my question.

"I need you to keep her walking," she said. "Check in with me by dawn and tell me how she's doing."

Dad went back to bed after that and so did my sister, Sarah-Kate, so it was just me and Mum after that. She made us toasted sandwiches and cups of tea and I walked Piper. I wouldn't let anyone else do it. I stayed up all night walking her in circles, and the kicking subsided. Mum just about had me convinced that we were over the worst of it, and we should go to bed too, when it all started up again. Worse, this time. She was thrashing on the ground, kicking and kicking.

This time the vet got to us in under an hour. As she examined Piper she looked much more serious than she had last night.

"I think we need to go to surgery," she said.

"What does that mean? What'll you do to her?" I asked.

"We'll put her under an anaesthetic and get her up on the operating table, and then make a cut along her underside on the belly from chest to tail so we can take the blockage out of her gut."

I tried not to think about Piper with her guts inside out.

"How much will it cost?" Mum asked. I knew what she was thinking – Piper wasn't insured.

"Including box rest afterwards? You won't get any change from $10,000. And it's major surgery. You need to factor in at least three months for the wound to heal on box rest."

"Will she compete again?" Mum asked.

"Depends," the vet sighed. "Some horses heal perfectly and they're back out there doing what they love. Others never come fully right. I can't give you guarantees. I'm sorry, surgery is still a risk."

"Is there another option?" Mum asked.

"At this stage?" the vet said. "If you want to keep her alive, there's no other option."

Mum looked at my face and she didn't hesitate. "Get Piper in the float, Hilly. We're taking her to surgery."

It's funny how quickly priorities change. Twenty-four hours ago, the most important thing in my world had been competing at the Open. Now, all that mattered was keeping Piper alive.

I remember sitting in the darkness as we drove that night, crying, and I felt Mum reach out to clutch my hand.

"I promise, Hilly, everything is going to be OK," she said. And when I didn't stop crying, that was when she said, "Maybe, instead of eventing this season, you should come with me to Iceland?"

Now, sitting in a Japanese restaurant on the other side of the world, that all seemed like a lifetime ago.

Dinner had been booked by Katherine's personal assistant, Lizzie, for twelve people. By the time that we turned up, most of the others had already arrived. I knew Jimmy, the assistant director – he was English but he'd worked in New Zealand a lot with Katherine. And Chris, the lighting guy, and Lizzie – they were old friends of Mum's from film school.

So there were ten of us already seated and waiting by the time Katherine arrived. Katherine wasn't one of those superstar directors who looked all Hollywood – she was just wearing a T-shirt and jeans. It was the woman beside her who was dressed as though she was famous. She had a really dramatic look about her with this flame-red Rapunzel hair. She wore this brilliant, floor-length purple patterned dress which looked incredible against her pale skin. Her eyes, a startling emerald green, seemed magnified behind her gigantic spectacles rimmed with red glitter frames.

"Everybody, I want to introduce you to Doctor Gudrun Gudmansdottir, professor of Norse mythology and Icelandic saga at Harvard University," Katherine had said. "I'm thrilled to have someone of her stature on board to ensure the integrity of this movie and help us to bring the real Princess Brunhilda to life."

Gudrun raised her hands in this spectral way, as if she were about to perform a séance or something, and then she reached out and picked up a champagne glass off the table and raised it to the light. "I have cast the runes and they tell me that the Norse gods will smile upon this production," she said theatrically. "Now join me in paying thanks to mighty Odin by raising your glasses and drinking deep in his honour!"

I could hear Mum mutter under her breath beside me as she reluctantly raised her glass. I caught her rolling her eyes at Jimmy as if to say, "Who is this nutter?"

"To mighty Odin!" Gudrun's toast was so loud the whole restaurant suddenly stopped talking. Draining her glass in one go, she put it back down, and then, rather than taking the empty seat beside Katherine, she walked the length of the table and made a beeline for me.

"I'll sit here. Bring me a chair…" She waved a hand airily at the waiter. Then she positioned herself in between me and Mum and locked me into the tractor beam of her powerful green eyes. She put her hand out to shake mine. I'd been expecting her skin to feel cold it was so white, but it was almost like touching fire.

"I'm Gudrun," she said.

"Hilly," I replied. "Hilly Harrison."

"Of course you are," Gudrun said, as if she knew this already. "You've travelled a long way, Hilly. Are you prepared for Iceland?"

"Oh, no!" I thought she had the wrong idea. "I mean, yes, I'm coming, but I'm not working as part of the crew or anything. I'm here with Mum."

Gudrun narrowed her eyes at me. "Do not underestimate yourself, Hilly. You have a role of your own to play. And a very important one it will be too."

She leaned close to me and whispered conspiratorially: "I threw the runes this morning and the gods told me everything. The future holds great adventure for us, Hilly. Ready yourself…"

"Excuse me—"

It was the waiter.

"What would you like to order, madam?"

Gudrun didn't open her menu, she just smiled up at him. "Do you have any puffin?"

The waiter looked horrified. "No, madam!"

Gudrun sighed with genuine disappointment. She turned to me. "It's so difficult to find puffin on the menu outside of Iceland. They're delicious roasted. The Icelanders catch them in butterfly nets."

Instead, Gudrun ordered the Atlantic salmon. I had the teriyaki chicken. As we ate, she asked me all about my life in Wellington and seemed genuinely excited when I told her that I rode.

"It must have been hard to leave your horse at home, to be away for so long?" Gudrun said.

I said nothing. I didn't want to talk about Piper.

"You'll find the Icelandic horses very different to the ones back home," Gudrun continued. "They're bred to be highly spirited and hot under saddle and they have five gaits."

I didn't understand. "Five gaits?"

"Most horses have just four gaits – they can walk, trot, canter and gallop," Gudrun replied. "An Icelandic horse has no gallop – instead they pace, and they have a fifth gait, the tölt, which is super fast – it's like a trot except it's so smooth you do not need to rise out of the saddle. When you ride a tölting horse, it feels like you're flying. You can sit on their backs quite comfortably like this for great distances."

"Have you ridden at a tölt?" I asked.

Gudrun smiled. "Of course. As a girl I grew up riding

every day. Everyone rides in Iceland. There are only three hundred thousand people, and there are a hundred thousand horses. The Icelandic has the purest blood of any horse in the world. Their breeding hasn't changed for a thousand years. They are the horses of the Vikings."

"So do you live in Reykjavik?" I asked.

Gudrun shook her head. "I grew up there, but New York's my home now. When Katherine asked me to work on this project, I knew I had to come back, though. *Brunhilda* is very important to me."

I had taken a look at the *Brunhilda* script when Mum was reading it on the plane. "So it's about the princess from *Sleeping Beauty*, right?"

Gudrun's face darkened. "*Sleeping Beauty* is a nonsense story! *Brunhilda* is not some fairy-tale princess. She was a real girl. This is precisely why I am here – so that this movie won't become some ridiculous recounting of her history, a helpless fawn waiting for a prince's kiss to awaken her. The true Brunhilda was the fiercest, the noblest of warriors, willing to fight to the ends of the earth for what she believed in. I have worked all my life to serve her truth."

Gudrun looked at me hard, her green eyes searching mine. "But why are you here, Hilly?"

I gulped down my sushi roll and thought about telling her everything about me and Piper and the worst time of my life, but in the end all I said was the truth.

"I didn't want to be home."

The flight to Iceland took us into Keflavik airport, an hour from the capital Reykjavik. We were picked up by three minivans and got on board with our bags before driving off in convoy. The landscape out of the window was like looking at Mars – plateaus of bare, rugged black rock patchworked with lichen, moss and snowdrifts with strange curls of smoke coming out of the ground.

"Steam not smoke," Mum corrected me when I pointed it out to her. "There are a hundred and thirty volcanoes here. Thirty of them are still active and even in summer there's snow. They call it the land of fire and ice."

We turned off the motorway not far from Keflavik because Lizzie thought it would be fun to stop for lunch at Blue Lagoon, a vast natural hot water lake.

"It's just so touristy," Gudrun said as we got out of the vans. "There's hot water everywhere in Iceland but this place is a little too crowded for me."

It smelled like the hot pools back home in Rotorua with a rotten tang of sulphur in the air. The hot water lake was huge and the water was an ice-cloudy blue.

Mum and I changed into our swimming costumes along with the crew and got in, sitting up to our armpits. Gudrun was off having an intense conversation with Katherine and didn't join us.

"Slip this on," Lizzie said, giving me a wristband.

"What's it for?" I asked.

"Anything you want!" She winked at me.

It was the coolest thing ever. All I had to do was wave my digital wristband at the kiosks and I was given whatever I wanted. Soft drinks, chips and hotdogs – well, Icelandic hotdogs, which were kind of like American ones but with this weird creamy mustard sauce. I asked for tomato sauce instead but even that was a little strange and tasted like sweet cheese.

We soaked in the pools until my skin wrinkled. It felt chalky and dried-out when we got back out and dressed in the cold air. Then we piled back into the vans, all toasty from the hot water.

Most tourists go to Reykjavik and stay there but we drove straight through. It wasn't a big city so it didn't take long and pretty soon it was like we were driving across a moonscape, all spooky and barren with scattered patches of snow despite the summer. Then, just as suddenly as it had appeared, the snow vanished and we were driving through tussocky plains, bare and desolate. It looked prehistoric here, almost as though humans had never existed.

We passed a roadside diner that looked closed except for the flashing lights that insisted it was open. By now it must have been late, but it was still eerily light. I looked at the time on the clock on the dashboard of the van: 11 p.m.

"There's the hotel." Mum nudged me and pointed off the main road to the right. In the far-off distance, I could see a long, low wooden lodge that looked like something the Vikings would have lived in except it was much bigger. It stood alone, in front of a massive forest of grey-green fir trees.

"So, that's our base for the next two months," Mum said.

The sign outside the hotel said ISBJÖRN. It translated as "ice bear" – polar bear, I guess it meant, since there was a giant stuffed polar bear standing on its hind legs in the foyer. Isbjörn had twelve rooms inside the lodge and another twenty-three cabins. The whole place had been rented out so that we were the only ones here. Katherine and the actors were going to be in the main lodge. The rest of us were allocated cabins around the grounds. Lizzie was methodically doing the rounds of the vans with a clipboard as everyone clamoured around her to find out where they were sleeping.

"Jillian, I've put you in the woods – total Hansel and Gretel job, little footpath into nowhere, but, trust me, it's very pretty..." Lizzie handed Mum our key on a wooden tag and a map of the hotel grounds.

"Which way?" Mum asked.

"Go through the hotel foyer," Lizzie called back without looking round. "Out the other side you'll see the path into the forest. Follow the middle track. On the map I gave you your cabin is marked with a red cross."

"You navigate, Hilly," Mum said, passing it to me.

I took the map and started reading. "We go this way," I said, pointing at the walk-through pavilion that divided the two main wings of the hotel.

The path was there. It split three ways and each artery was signposted for cabins three, four and five.

"That's us, cabin five." I led the way.

Mum was already on her phone, talking to Nicky, her assistant, who was arriving tomorrow with the costumes. Some of the cast were on Nicky's flight but the main actors and actresses weren't due to arrive for two more weeks. Mum had already done fittings for all of them, but there were still details to go through and more clothes to source. She wanted to have everything on hand to do final fittings before shooting began. I could hear Nicky's voice on the other end of the phone, all shrill and panicky. She was saying there were problems getting the suits of armour through UK customs. The customs officer thought the shoulder pads with the spikes should be classified as weapons. Mum was so calm as she advised her what to do – it made me realise how good she was at her job. The other night at dinner, when Katherine had introduced everyone to Gudrun, she had referred to Mum as the "Oscar-award-winning costume designer Jillian Harrison". Mum didn't care about her Oscar – she was currently using it to prop open the cat flap at home – but it made me feel proud.

"No bars. I need to backtrack," she said suddenly, holding her phone up above her head, searching for a signal. "I have to clear this up now. You keep on going, Hilly. I'll catch you up at the cabin."

It was like something out of a movie in that forest. The trees around me were so damp they dripped water. Bright green moss grew on the trunks on the dark side where no light could reach it. I walked slowly at first, thinking Mum might catch me up, but then I got cold and my fingers were numb so I sped up again, and then I saw the little red toadstool on the ground. Not natural but manmade with a sign beside it, an arrow made out of wood with the number five on it that pointed in the direction of our cabin.

When I look back on what happened next, I still can't figure out how she did it. I remember we were all waiting by the minivans when Lizzie gave us our keys and allocated our rooms. Mum and I had set off down the path to our cabin straight away after that. I hadn't seen anybody else come this way. So how was it that Gudrun was already on the doorstep of the cabin, sitting on a rocking chair and waiting for me?

She jumped straight up, an air of impatience about her, as if she'd been there for hours.

"Throw your bags inside quickly, Hilly," she said. "We need to hurry."

"But…" I was confused. "Mum's still back there. She's on the phone."

But Gudrun ignored me. As I put the key in the lock, she turned the handle for me, then helped me to put my bags in the room. I only just had time to look around and see the shadowy shapes of deer antlers hanging on the walls before she had bustled me back out again and we were walking on the path that took us deeper into the forest.

Gudrun walked so fast I was panting with the effort as I skipped to catch up with her.

We walked like this, saying nothing for a little way. Just when I was about to summon up the courage to ask her where we were going, the woods cleared in front of us and we were obviously in the place she wanted me to see.

Years ago when I was little we'd taken a family holiday to Rome and visited the Colosseum. I remember standing at the side and staring down into the depths of it and imagining all those fights to the death on the sand between the gladiators with their swords and tridents, and the wild tigers and lions being let loose to eat the Christians.

This place we were in now was like a miniature version of that, a circular structure of stone steps sinking down into the earth to create an enclosed arena. Not big enough for the colosseum, but still pretty big. I couldn't figure out whether it was natural or man-made – the stone steps were covered in grass. Gudrun began to vault down them towards the arena. She was carrying a tote bag across her back and it bounced as she leapt, making a clattering noise like it had bells inside.

I clambered after her, tentatively taking the first step in an ungainly fashion, before figuring out that the best way to get down was to do what Gudrun was doing and leap and land then leap again. Finally I reached the bottom too – not sand like the real Colosseum but dry tussock grass. Gudrun strode out until she was standing right in the middle of the arena and began pulling items out of her bag, including a garden trowel.

"Here!" she called to me. "Come and help me to dig."

I did as she asked and dug, chipping away at the hard crust beneath the grassy surface. It was tough at first but, once I'd broken through, it crumbled away more easily and soon I'd made a decent hole, with a mound of earth beside it.

"That will do," Gudrun said. She was still fossicking in her bag.

"Gudrun?" I finally summoned up the nerve. "What are we doing?"

"We're preparing," she replied, pulling out a cow's horn from her bag and laying it down next to the hole.

"Soon it will be the Jonsmessa – the apex of midsummer," Gudrun said. "In ancient Iceland this was considered a most magical time. And so, to honour the ancients, we prepare for the ritual. We will bury this horn now and then, when the time is right, we will return."

Gudrun produced a bundle of purple herbs and some yellow flowers, shoving half of them into the cow's horn before turning to me. "May I have your necklace please?"

There was a silver chain around my neck that Mum had given me for my birthday. I hesitated. "My necklace? Why?"

Gudrun sighed. "The ritual requires something that has touched your flesh."

I frowned. "Will I get it back again?"

"Yes, of course," Gudrun said, as if she'd made this obvious already. "We will return for it."

I took the necklace off and I was about to hand it to her but she shrank back. "No," she instructed. "Not to me. You must put it in the horn."

So I slipped the necklace inside, on top of the purple herbs, and then Gudrun took some more yellow flowers and pushed them into the horn too. Then she laid the horn carefully on its side in the hole I'd dug before patting the soil flat back over it.

She beckoned for me to stand up again. She stood beside me, her eyes closed and her hands raised above her head, and chanted a verse in a language I didn't recognise. When she opened her eyes again she was smiling at me.

"All done," she said brightly. "You can go home now, Hilly. Your mother will be wondering where you are."

It was true. Mum was already waiting for me when I got back. When she asked where I had been, I knew it would wind her up if I mentioned Gudrun. Mum clearly found her annoying already. So I just said I'd gone for a look around while she finished her call.

In our cabin that night, I slept really well because I was so jetlagged. I didn't notice that the night sky was as bright as day. When I woke up, the clock said it was morning, although time seemed meaningless by then.

For a moment, I couldn't work out how I'd even ended up here, and when I thought back to the whole episode in the Colosseum with Gudrun, it felt so surreal I could have sworn I'd imagined it. But then I put my hand to my neck and realised, with a shiver, that my silver chain was gone.

CHAPTER 3

Transmogrification

We were having breakfast in the hotel restaurant the next morning when Gudrun swept in, red curls flying out behind her in a fiery blaze.

"I've just read the new script." She flung the thick wodge of paper down in front of me and it hit the table with a dull thud.

"Is it any good?" I asked.

"Aargh." Gudrun pulled a face. "If you like fairy tales, it's excellent. But I'm not interested in fairy tales. It's the truth that I want to see. The real Brunhilda, a ferocious warrior who takes the throne after her father and leads her tribe to be Queen of Iceland."

I must have looked doubtful because Gudrun picked up on my hesitation.

"Isn't this what you want too, Hilly?"

"Yes, I guess," I said, "if that's the truth, but what I want doesn't necessarily count around here."

Gudrun's eyes narrowed. "But what do you think?"

I sat there for a moment, gathering my thoughts so that I would say this right. "Why is it that in all the movies I see the Vikings are men? I've never seen a girl Viking. Maybe the girls really did just cook and clean and the boys were the only ones who got to do all the cool stuff like swordfights and horse riding."

"You see history as it's told by men," Gudrun said. "And these men know nothing because they weren't there."

"I guess so," I replied, "but you weren't there either. The only person who really knows what happened to her is Brunhilda."

I thought Gudrun would be cross with me for saying this. But she looked delighted and threw her arms around me.

"Exactly! Oh, I knew I was right to choose you!" She gave me a kiss on the forehead.

I wasn't sure exactly what she was going on about, but I smiled anyway.

"Two weeks from tonight, Jonsmessa will be here at

last," she went on. "Then, Hilly, we'll find out everything we need to know."

There was even more bounce than usual to her step as she headed back out the door, dashing past Mum, who was heading to our table from the breakfast buffet with a plate of bacon and eggs for us both.

"What's up with Gudrun?" she asked.

"What do you mean?" My heart was racing.

"She came in and left again without eating anything." Mum shook her head. "That woman is very peculiar."

"Yes," I agreed, "she most certainly is."

In the weeks of pre-production that followed, Gudrun didn't mention Jonsmessa again to me. She was still pretty friendly, but her focus seemed to be on Katherine and the script and getting it right. They would frequently sit at a table in the dining room locked in heated discussions. Sometimes I would see Gudrun by herself at the same table late into the evenings as she cast her runes and chanted. One morning at breakfast, before we ate she'd insisted the room needed "cleansing" and we had to wait to eat until she could perform her ritual:

waving a burning bunch of sage. Considering the frequent strangeness of her behaviour, being dragged along to bury a cow's horn didn't seem so out of the ordinary when I thought about it now. In fact, it had pretty much become a distant memory. Also, I had something else to distract me from the cultural consultant's enchantments. I had somehow landed myself a job.

It had happened the same morning that Gudrun had cleansed the room at breakfast. Mum was sorting out the room in the hotel that she'd been allocated for costume storage. Mum's assistant had gone back to London for more items and was due to return that afternoon, and they were on the phone to each other talking about how many racks they needed when there was a knock at the door. I opened it to find a woman with sandy blonde hair tied back in a messy plait. She was wearing jodhpurs and riding boots.

"I'm Niamh," she said. "I'm from the equine department. I'm afraid we have a problem."

"What kind of a problem?" Mum asked.

Niamh pulled a face. "It's easier if I show you... Let's go to the stables."

The stables turned out to be a low block of buildings,

36

just a short walk from the hotel, down by the river. I was shocked at the enormity of the scale of them. There were so many rows of loose boxes! And there was an indoor training ménage with a round pen and a sawdust schooling arena too.

"It's so lucky they had these facilities here for your horses," I said as Niamh slid back the barn doors.

"Oh no," she laughed. "None of this existed before. They custom-built it for us so that it was ready when we got here. The weather was so cold and wet when we arrived. It was the middle of winter – minus fifteen degrees and pitch black outside most days. We were getting up in the dark and working all day in the dark – our lives had almost no daylight for months really. The weather back home in Ireland isn't great but at least there's sun! So naturally under those conditions we were really looking forward to summer. We didn't think about the major problem it would cause."

"What problem?" Mum asked.

"I'll show you," Niamh said.

We walked up the central corridor of the stable block and Niamh went up to the loose box that was labelled in gold with the name OLAFUR.

"This is Olafur, but we call him Ollie." Niamh opened

the top half of the Dutch door. There was a horse inside, standing in the middle of the loose box. He had the look of a prize fighter, stocky and burly, yet he was no more than fifteen hands high. His eyes, which were half-closed as if he had been dozing, were almost completely covered by an enormous bushy forelock. It looked like he had a massive fringe, this giant explosion of sunburnt brown hair that sprang out from between his ears and then crested his powerful neck. His tail was bushy and enormous too, and had the same bedraggled sunburnt colour against his coat, which was quite sleek and almost black.

"What breed is he?" I asked.

"He's an Icelandic," Niamh said. "They all are. Connor, that's my brother, he and I wanted to bring our own stunt horses with us from Ireland, but the rules are strict and it's impossible to bring any horses in."

"Why?"

"It's been the law for centuries now." Niamh shook her head in wonder. "They're really serious about keeping the bloodlines of their horses pure. And if you take an Icelandic horse out of the country, even for a single day to compete or for work, that's the end of it. They're not allowed to return again. Ever."

"Really?"

"Banished for life," Niamh confirmed.

"So, because of this law, you couldn't bring any of your own trained horses here, then?" Mum said.

"Nope." Niamh sighed. "Which put us on the back foot. We've had to train all of these new horses since we arrived in winter. And the whole time we were sending photos back to the production team of the horses we'd bought for schooling and Katherine was so excited. She loved the way they appeared so rugged with their coats all long and sun-bleached and shaggy." Niamh seemed like she was about to burst into tears. "And then, just before filming started, summer arrived, and now look!" She waved a dismissive hand at Ollie, standing sleek and black before her. "It's a nightmare! They're all like this!"

"So they've moulted to their summer coats and lost their shaggy winter fur?" Mum grasped the situation. "And what do you want me to do?"

"I want," Niamh said, "I want you to make it winter again."

Mum didn't bat an eye at the craziness of Niamh's request. She stared hard at Ollie for a moment and then she dialled her phone. "Nicky? It's me. Where are

39

you? The airport? You've finally arrived? Good. OK, I'm going to give you the number of a contact in Reykjavik. I need you to go pick up some goat hair."

A few hours later, Nicky was at the hotel with a minivan filled with six commercial bales of coarse-strand goat hair.

This was how Mum made the horse suits. Handfuls of the goat hair were dyed just the right shade of brown and then the ends were bleached to look like they'd been out in the sun. The hair was hand-stitched onto sheer black mesh which had been sewn with a zip that went from jaw to tail beneath the belly of the horse, in much the same way that a human might wear a onesie. A Velcro attachment hooked up onto the bridle to hold the suit in place at one end and tail clips fixed it at the other so that once it was done up there was no way to tell it was there and the goat hair looked exactly like the horse's own natural long, shaggy winter coat.

Fashioning the horse-onesie was tricky work. The costumes had to be fitted perfectly to each individual horse. And that was where I came in. It was a two-man job to take precise measurements, involving one person making notes and the other lying down on the ground with a tape measure to chart the dimensions of their belly and combine this with their length all the way from their head to beneath the dock of their tail.

Mum and Nicky's domain was the sewing room, where they had their team cutting and stitching the suits, and I stayed at the stables helping Niamh.

We did forty horses together. I would spend hours lying on my back beneath the bellies of the stallions with Niamh bent down beside me writing down the measurements that I gave her. By the time we were done I knew everything about her. She was eighteen, so only five years older than me, and had left school as soon as she could to go to work for her brother Connor who ran Equus Films.

"Horses are in the blood," Niamh had said. "Mum and Dad breed point-to-point racers. Connor and I were both in the Irish National team for Pony Club Mounted Games. We're both daredevils – the stunts we do now started out as things we did at home, like teaching our ponies to bow and rear, or swinging onto their backs off ropes and galloping them bareback."

Mark, the third member of the team, was Irish too, a friend of Connor's from Pony Club days.

"He and Connor started the company together before I joined, so that makes them the bosses," Niamh explained. "Connor does most of the ridden work. He's been training the two lead stallions, Troy and Ollie. Ollie is going to be the horse that the prince rides. He needs to be able to do all the usual stunts – you know, drop to one knee and rear on cue, and he also has to jump through fire to do the rescue at the end of the film. Troy has to do stunts too, but he's also got to act because there are lots of scenes with him and Brunhilda together, so we need a horse that has presence, you know? Like a movie star."

Considering he was supposed to be a movie star, Troy was not at all what I'd been expecting. He was handsome enough – a deep russet chestnut with a flaxen mane – and he was beautiful, almost feminine for a stallion. I guess he was the right horse for a princess, but he wasn't quite what I'd pictured when Gudrun had talked about Jotun, Brunhilda's famous stallion. If Brunhilda really was this ferocious warrior, then Troy seemed a bit tame for her. Not that I said this to Niamh, of course, who was totally in love with Troy.

"Don't you think Jam is going to look amazing on him?" she said as she groomed his thick, shaggy blond mane.

"Jam?"

Niamh looked at me as if I were from another planet. "Jamisen O'Brien. She's playing Brunhilda. You must know her! She was in that Hollywood blockbuster last summer – the musical one set in Greece."

"Oh," I said, slightly embarrassed that I hadn't clicked immediately when Niamh called her Jam. "Yeah, of course I know her. I used to love her TV show."

"Jamisen's an amazing horsewoman," Niamh continued. "She'll be riding all her own stunts. The costume department have this enormous long blonde wig that she wears under her Viking helmet and it will look incredible blowing in the wind next to Troy's flaxen mane."

"It must be weird," I said, "to be not that much older than me and be the star of an entire movie."

"She's used to it, I guess," Niamh said. "What is she now? Sixteen? She's been famous almost her whole life."

The arrival of Jamisen O'Brien and Anders Mortenson had everyone talking at dinner. The two stars of the film had finally turned up on a private jet with their entourages in tow, ready to start work the next day.

"Jam's brought six assistants with her," Niamh told me as we piled up our plates at the buffet.

My mum had worked on a lot of films and she'd told me some stories but I swear I'd never heard of any celebrity who had that many assistants before.

"What do they all do?" I asked.

"One of them is her personal trainer, one of them is her hairdresser, one of them is her personal assistant…" Niamh rattled them off, counting on her fingers. "Don't know what the others do."

Anders Mortenson, on the other hand, had just his personal assistant with him. He'd been famous since he was ten years old when he played a spoilt rich kid in the TV comedy *Cody and Toby* and now, at the age of fifteen, this was the first time he'd play the hero. He was Prince Sigard, who would fight by Brunhilda's side as her power grew and eventually marry his queen.

"They get here today and then it's a week of training with us and the stunt co-ordinators," Niamh explained, "and then filming will finally begin…"

The sudden hush that fell over the dining room at that moment made me think that maybe Jam and Anders had just walked in. But it was only Gudrun. She stood out from the rest of us in our North Face puffer jackets at the best of times, but today she was particularly wildly dressed in red trousers and a violet cape.

She made a beeline for our table and flung herself down beside me.

"Hilly, we need to talk."

I saw Niamh tense up in her presence. She couldn't stand Gudrun; she'd admitted that to me when we'd been working on the goat-hair suits together.

"Don't you think it's weird how she always talks to you?" Niamh had said to me once when she was going on about Gudrun's odd behaviour.

It was true and, yes, I did think it was a bit strange. I was the least important person here and yet Gudrun treated me like someone who really mattered. It made me uneasy but I kind of liked talking to her too.

Niamh stood up to leave. "I have to go. Hilly, let's meet up at the stables in half an hour, OK?"

"Sure," I said.

Gudrun waited in silence until Niamh was out of earshot. Her green eyes were even wilder and brighter than usual.

"Do you know what night it is, Hilly?"

"Sunday?" I offered.

"Yes," Gudrun conceded. "Sunday, the 24th of June. The Jonsmessa is here at last. It's time."

Then she leaned closer so that she could whisper to me: "I'll come for you just before midnight. We must finish what we've started. It's time to meet Brunhilda."

That night I sat up on my bed, fully dressed, waiting for Gudrun. She said the ritual needed to take place at midnight but by 11.30 p.m. she still wasn't here. Finally at around 11.45 p.m. I gave up on her and closed the blackout curtains in my room. I had only just started to get ready for bed when I heard this scratching on the glass of the sliding door. Then another sound, a thin, melancholic whimper. I sat bolt upright and listened. More whimpering, louder this time. I got up, and moved cautiously over to the window and flung the curtains apart.

In front of me, right on the other side of the glass door, stood two enormous grey wolves. They were standing there, side by side, like two statues, eyes blazing intently, tongues lolling from their massive open jaws.

We were separated by the glass, so they couldn't get to me, but that didn't make them any less terrifying.

I put my hand up to the pane and one of the wolves edged closer. His breath steamed the glass and I could see saliva dripping from his white fangs. The other one cocked his head and moved forward too. They were massive, powerful creatures, and I was sure at that moment that if they'd wanted to they could have broken down the glass to get to me. But they didn't try. They didn't even growl. They both stared intently at me. Then, as if they'd heard someone calling them, they turned on their heels and bounded away, into the forest. A moment later, another shape emerged from the shadows of the trees. It was Gudrun! I slid the door open for her.

"Quick!" I hissed. "Get inside! There are wolves out there."

Gudrun was perfectly calm. "There are no wolves in Iceland," she said.

"I know what I saw," I insisted. I wanted her to come in so I could shut the door, but she beckoned me outside instead.

"Seriously, Hilly," she said. "There's nothing there. Come on. It's time. We need to go."

I didn't want to stay there arguing and risk waking Mum and so I stepped outside and slid the door shut behind me.

We walked to the Colosseum, Gudrun leading the way. The sky up above was cloudless, and the colour of rose petals.

"Quick, Hilly!" Gudrun leapt ahead of me, taking the stone steps two at a time to reach the grassy expanse of the arena. She grasped my hand and shoved the trowel into it. "Dig up the horn while I prepare."

The dirt mound from our burial had become overgrown with grass, which surprised me as it seemed like such a short time ago we had done the ritual. Gudrun must have marked the spot somehow because she was quite certain where I should dig.

A few feet away she had placed a fire brazier stacked with logs.

"The Vikings always used mountain ash, from the boughs of the rowan tree, for the midsummer ritual," she said as she rearranged the wood inside the bowl of the rusty brazier and set it alight with a taper. "They believed that rowan has magical properties to ward off evil."

The wood caught fire almost instantly with a fairy

dust sprinkling of orange sparks at first and then a deep, emerald-green flame as the rowan began to burn and crackle to embers. There was something very hypnotic about watching the fire, almost trance-like.

"Hilly!" Gudrun said. "Please, keep digging – it's time!"

I plunged the trowel back into the earth and heard a *thunk* as it struck bone.

"I've got it!" I said, using my fingers to prise the horn out of the soil, wiping it clean. I expected the herbs inside to have rotted away but the flowers were still brilliant yellow and the leaves were still green. I was about to reach in and get my necklace out when Gudrun stopped me.

"Be very careful with it. You must not disturb its contents as you bring it to me."

I held the horn as if it were a baby in my arms and walked to Gudrun, who was stoking the wood with an iron so that the green flames leapt up as tall as me. It was strange, but there was no warmth emanating from the fire. It was as cold as ice.

Gudrun stood and took the horn from me. "You kneel," she said.

I dropped to my knees next to the brazier. Gudrun

lowered her hands into the green flames and rested the horn on top of the logs. All at once the fire changed colour, first to brilliant pink, then to gold.

"Look into it," Gudrun said to me. "Tell me what you see."

I stared at the flames. Suddenly, in their flicker, shapes emerged. I was getting really weirded-out now, but the fire held me steady, entranced in its flames. "I see the two wolves," I said to Gudrun, "the same ones who came to me earlier. But they are with a man this time. He's very tall and very old."

"And his face?" Gudrun asked me.

I looked hard at his face and I saw that on one side there was a black pit where an eye had once been.

"He's got one eye," I said. "And a long beard and there are these birds; big, black crows. They sit on his shoulders."

"They are ravens, not crows," Gudrun said. "Hugin and Munin – Thought and Memory. And his wolves, the ones you saw earlier, are Geri and Freki. They are his constant companions. I knew you were special, Hilly, the first moment I met you."

"Who is he?" I asked.

"Odin," she replied, as if this were obvious. "The

All-Father. Greatest of all the Norse gods. Odin, who decides which warriors are honourable enough to lift up after death to sit at his side at the feasting table in his heaven, Valhalla. He is here with us now. This is a good sign. We can begin the ritual."

And with that she produced a bunch of sage from her robes, lit the tips of it in the fire and began to move around me in a circle, chanting. The flames were mesmerising, licking up and then falling away to low-burning embers. The vision of Odin, his wolves and his ravens had disappeared and I looked up and saw blue eyes staring back at me from the fire, a girl no older than me, with blonde hair in tight braids.

She reached out a hand to me and my pulse quickened as Gudrun stepped forward to the brazier. Putting her hands directly into the embers, she pulled out the horn. The flames had turned it white, and now there were carvings in the bone surface – intricate patterns and symbols like the runes that Gudrun kept in her velvet bag. She reached inside the horn and pulled out my silver chain and beckoned me to her so that she could clasp it back around my neck. Even though it had been in the heat of the fire just a moment before, the filigree felt like ice at my throat.

"From ancient times, we bring you forth, Brunhilda. Let the exchange be complete so that we may know your truth!"

Gudrun tossed the bundle of burning sage into the flames and it exploded in a burst of golden sparks.

"Springa!" she cried out as the fire leapt once more. And even though she was speaking ancient Norse, this time I knew somehow that the word meant *Jump!*

Inside me, my spirit soared and left my body and suddenly I was in the flames, the fire so brilliant all around that it blinded me.

Later, when Gudrun explained to me how the Cross-Over had happened, how she had "transmogrified me into Brunhilda" as she transported me back through the fire, I would understand more deeply what had happened. At that moment though, as I felt myself shift shapes, I had no idea about transmogrification and no way to explain it. All I knew was that somehow I wasn't Hilly Harrison any more.

And when I opened my eyes, the stone steps of the Colosseum were no longer empty – they were filled with people and horses. Two stallions, one pale grey, the other a chestnut. Both had their ears flattened back in anger, squealing and threatening each other with teeth bared. The men who held them tried to avoid being hurt as the horses reared up and lashed out with their hooves. The men were struggling to restrain them as they fastened the ropes to bind the horses together.

At last they had tied the final knot and the horses, now bound to each other, were let loose. As soon as the horses realised they were free from the men's grasp, they turned their attention on each other. They rose up on their hind legs, hooves thrashing the air, and then, with a battle scream, the grey horse lunged to attack. As he bit into the neck of the chestnut, there were cheers from the crowd.

It was a horse fight! I couldn't watch. I turned from the arena and ran. I was sobbing so hard I could barely breathe and the tears blurred my vision so that I couldn't really see where I was going and then with a hard thud I was stopped in my tracks. I had run right into something. No. I'd run into some*one*.

A giant of a man was standing before me. His head was shaved right up the sides but he still sported a thick, full red beard. On his head where the hair had been shaved off he was tattooed with the symbols of the runes. He wore ragged clothes, but the golden bracelets that decorated his bulging arms showed that he was a man of power and influence, a chief, a king.

With a massive hand on each of my slight shoulders he grasped me and held me out from him as if to examine me, before he pulled me hard to crush me against his chest, embracing me in a hug. He held me so tight he choked the breath out of me as he said my name:

"*Brunhilda.*"

I smiled as I gazed up at him.

I had never seen him before in my life and yet I knew exactly who he was.

"Hello, Father."

CHAPTER 4

The All-Thing

My father holds me by the shoulders and lifts me off the ground.

"Where are you running off to then, little one?" he asks. "The entertainments are in the other direction."

I squirm, trying to relocate my feet back on the earth once more, feeling ridiculous dangling there from his gigantic paws.

In the pit behind me I hear the horses as they clash, their squeals mingling with the cries of excitement from the men gathered round them.

"I feel sick," I tell him. I don't say why. He would never understand my revulsion at this theatre of brutality. His life is all about bloodshed. How many thousands of men has he killed in his long boat raids?

Their lives mean nothing to him, so how can I possibly explain my floods of tears, my distress over the death of a horse?

My father raises me up even further off the ground, holding me fast so that I'm looking him square in the eyes.

"You're hungry, I think," he says as if his proclamation settles the problem. "Never mind. The feast will be soon enough. Until then you will stay with me."

He puts me back on the ground but he doesn't remove his hands from my shoulders. He turns me round and shuffles me off to walk ahead of him. When we reach the arena, he puts his arm protectively round me from behind as we push through the throng, back the way I've just come, creating a pathway through the crowd-stink of sweat and beer, into the arena seats, where the noise of the people shouting all around is deafening.

An almighty roar rises up as the chestnut stallion, exhausted and lame with open wounds on his shoulder and neck, suddenly summons up the strength to land a glancing blow with his near fore. The grey reacts like a snake, twisting his neck to wrap it round the chestnut's and bite him back. The chestnut falls back, trying to get away from the grey, and once again he finds himself restrained by the ropes that bind them together, unable to escape.

I'm trapped here too. A prisoner, with my own father as jailer. All I can do to get through it is close my eyes and bite my tongue and wait for this "entertainment" to end.

"Where is your brother?" my father asks.

"I don't know," I say. I haven't seen Steen all day. I'm new to having a brother, but instinctively I know that I do not like him. I'm thinking about last night, and I know it can't be *my* memory; it must be Brunhilda's I suppose. It involves Steen and the dinner feast we had at Thing-Vellir. One of our tribe had just got married and so the bride and groom were guests of honour and there was much celebrating at the main table, and Steen leant across to me and whispered:

"That will be you next, sister."

He's so cruel! I don't want to marry at all but there's a queue of boys in my tribe lining up in anticipation of standing on the sacred rock and having their hand roped to mine. Not for love, but because of the power it would bring them. My father is the strongest of the chieftains,

King of Iceland. Marrying me, Brunhilda, his daughter, gives you a direct line to the throne.

All the same, Steen would be wise not to mock me. "Be careful what you wish for, brother," I replied. "If I do marry, then my husband could be the next king instead of you."

I swear he had not even considered this. He turned very pale when I said it. Honestly, my brother is like Thor. Full of power and fury, always ready to swing a hammer, but never once using his brain. He never thinks before he acts, and that is why he should not be king.

The roar of the crowd is growing louder as the horses, entangled in the ropes, stagger about like punch-drunk fighters, weaving and striking. The chestnut stumbles forward and falls to his knees. I think I'm going to throw up.

"Brunhilda, go now and find him for me," my father says. "I want him at the feast tonight when I address the chieftains at the Law Rock."

"Yes, Father!"

I don't wait to be told twice – I move fast, pushing my way out through the crowd. Oh, thank the great, wise Odin! I'm so relieved to have an excuse to leave. I can feel my heart pounding but I try to stay calm as I work my way between the stinking bodies of the men who are shouting at the top of their lungs. Being small has its uses and I weave through the gaps in the throng until I've left the noise and the stench behind me and I'm heading down the broad path that leads between the high rock cliffs towards the far end of Thing-Vellir.

I know where Steen likes to hang out and, sure enough, I find him in one of the little clearings, a rocky cul-de-sac where the waterfalls tumble down the cliff face. He's there with a few boys and girls from our tribe. He has his sword in his hand and he's fighting with Kari, his best friend. They play with blunted blades, dulled on purpose for sparring so they will not cut, although you can get a nasty bruise through your chain mail if you're hit hard enough with one.

Steen and Kari are trading blows back and forth in a very choreographed way while the others sit above them on the rocks and watch. I think, as I watch him grunting and thrusting, blocking Kari with his shield and then grinning as he swoops around with his sword to hack at his shoulder, how Steen fights like a poor imitation of our father, his arms windmilling and his chest jutting forward. He is built like my father too, only smaller in height. He's sixteen, two years older than me, and his beard is not yet grown and is still just a tuft of ginger fluff on his chin.

When he sees me he doesn't pause, he keeps clashing his sword against Kari's.

"Why are you here, Bru?"

"Father wanted me to find you," I tell him. "The feast is soon. He wants to make sure you'll be there."

"Of course he does." Steen thrusts his sword hard at Kari and even though they are just playing he only narrowly misses striking him in the guts. Kari looks nervous.

"Hey! Watch it!"

"He's going to announce it tonight," Steen says. "Wait and see."

"Announce what?" I ask.

"His successor," Steen says. "He's an old man now. Time to move aside and let a young man take over."

"You better not let him hear you say he's old," I say, "or the sword he uses on you will be a real one. Anyway, even if he's announcing his successor, what makes you so certain it will be you?"

Steen stops fighting suddenly and lets his sword drop. He raises a hand to Kari as if to say, "Hold fast and halt a moment?" Then he turns his back on Kari and he glares at me.

"My father is the king," he says to me. "And his father before him was king."

I smile at the arrogance of him.

"My father is also the king," I point out. "And where is it written that a woman cannot rule? The strongest warrior is the one who takes charge of our tribe. Father is not handing down the crown to the first boy who happened to be born."

"The warrior is always a boy," Steen counters.

I laugh. "I can hunt better than you and ride better than you. I'm smarter than you too."

From the rocks above us there's giggling. Steen looks up to see his friends smirking at him being bested in words by his little sister.

"Is that so?" He's not laughing. He walks over to Kari. "Let me have your sword," he says. Kari hesitates and Steen loses his temper, shouting at him: "Your sword, Kari! Let me have it now!"

Kari shifts his hand down the hilt and offers it out so that Steen can take it from him.

Steen now has a sword in each hand as he walks to me.

"And can you fight as well as I can?" he asks. He offers me Kari's sword. "Because if you can beat me right now, then I will go to Father and tell him it should be you and not me who is to take over when he steps aside as king."

"I will need chain mail or the fight is not fair," I point out.

"Kari?" My brother treats his friends as if they are servants the way he speaks to them, which is another reason why he should never be king. I stand and wait as Kari wriggles out of his chain mail and hands it to me too. He's much bigger than me and when I pull it on over my clothes it sags off my shoulders.

I put out my hand to take Kari's sword from Steen and as I do so I note the slenderness of my own wrist. I am like a sparrow! My bones are so narrow and tiny beside Steen's heavy hands. When I feel the heft of the sword as I take it from him, my arm starts trembling and I have to hook my elbow in to my hip for support and pretend that I'm holding it naturally so that he doesn't see this. I step back from him and deliberately let the sword fall down so that the point is lowered to rest on the ground. And then, taking a deep breath, I square off and step my feet into position, my posture erect, and with renewed strength I raise the sword up so that it's squared to the centre of my body, sticking out directly in front of me. On my left side my shield is so heavy I feel my muscles quivering. Let the fight begin *soon please*, because my arms already cannot last any longer.

"Let's do this," I say.

When we were little, Steen and I would sometimes spend the day together trapping birds beneath a basket using a string and a dowel. Steen would only wait until the birds were barely underneath the basket and eating the breadcrumbs, and then he'd give this warlike roar and throw himself at it to push it down over them. Of course they would hear him coming and be gone long before he could reach the basket. He was always astonished when he looked through the wicker and saw it was empty.

He will be the same today in the fight – impatient and half-witted. To win, all I have to do is use these traits against him.

And so I stand back and let him make the first move and, sure enough, with a growl he lunges right at me, front foot first, hacking and waving his sword theatrically above his head, all bluster and forewarning so that I see him coming in plenty of time – and all it takes is for me to sidestep and I'm clear. I slash crossways and take the first strike against him, whacking my brother hard in the ribs.

"Oww!" Steen is furious as he staggers to one side. He's still trying to regain his balance when I come at him again, acting fast, my sword in front of me, shield raised to protect my vulnerable neck and shoulder. *Hack-hack-hack.* I swing and this time I land three successive blows onto his left shoulder until finally he gets his shield up to block me and fights back with a cross-cut which I deftly block with my own weapon and then push his sword out and away from my body with my blade. I twist myself in a knot to slip inside of him, throwing the weight of my shield into his and pushing hard. Caught off-balance, Steen is tipped over on his back like a turtle and, before he knows what's happening, I'm on top of him and my blade tip is in the soft groove where his throat meets his neck.

I can see his pulse in that groove, the beat of his heart pounding, throbbing through his skin. There's sweat on his upper lip.

All it would take from me now is one thrust, even with

a sword as blunt as this, and there would be no question of succession. I would end his life. Our eyes lock and I give him a knowing raise of my eyebrow. I stay there, sitting on his chest, and wait a heartbeat longer before I lower my sword. I put it back in its sheath and as soon as I do this Steen gives a furious roar and pushes me off him. I fall back on the grass laughing.

"You can stop gloating!" he shouts at me. "You got lucky is all!"

"Well done, Bru!"

I look up and see my friends Astrid and Hannecke. They're cheering for me from the rocks above. Even the boys, who should be on Steen's side, are hooting out in glee. But Steen isn't laughing. He lies on his back in a sulk, refusing my hand when I offer it to help him up. Finally he takes it, but then as soon as he's on his feet he snatches my sword and throws it up to Kari.

"This changes nothing," he mutters darkly. "You know that, don't you?"

I look at him and shake my head with pity. I knew he wouldn't keep the deal. "See you tonight at dinner," I say. And then I turn and walk away.

65

Our journey to reach Thing-Vellir for the great meeting of the tribes has not been long. My father is chieftain in the south, not far from here, and we followed the river, travelling for a day. The men of our tribe and many families have come too, almost a hundred of us, all on horseback. The six other tribes who join us have come from across the country and for many their journey has taken weeks. They all travel by horse as we do, men, women and children riding astride. It's the only way here because the few tracks that cross the lands are too bumpy and rutted for a carriage to be of any use.

So as well as thousands of people, there are thousands of horses too at the All-Thing, the great conference of all the tribes of Iceland. There has been much trading and selling of stallions, mares and foals between us since we arrived and my father has been asked many times since we got here about my horse, Jotun.

Jotun is the handsomest stallion in the whole of Iceland. I'm not saying this just because he's mine. It's the truth.

It wasn't always the case. As a small foal, Jotun wasn't good-looking at all. His legs were too long and he had a big head, so that when I chose him my father asked me if I was sure and whether I wouldn't rather choose another colt with more attractive looks and better conformation.

"He is the one I want," I had said firmly.

By the time Jotun was three he was still gangly but he was enormous, almost fifteen two hands high.

I wanted to ride him then, but I held back and waited for him and watched him at liberty in the fields when he played with the other colts. I knew from back then that he was a true Icelandic horse and possessed all five gaits. Without a rider on his back he would already tölt and pace. I couldn't wait to saddle-train him so that I could feel the smoothness of his strides.

At four years old, his muscles finally filled out and he was magnificent. His mane and tail, which had been almost blond when he was young, had turned their true colour and were as brilliant as wildfire. It was under saddle though that Jotun truly transformed from this sweet, playful pony into a stallion with the fire and brimstone of a volcano. His reactions were swift and furious and he took my breath away with every stride. On his back at the age of ten, I learned what it meant to wield power. And I knew I wanted that.

Jotun is the best horse in all of Iceland – and he's

mine, and only mine. That is another reason, as if he needed one, for Steen to hate me.

On the plains, all of the tribes' horses graze together, gathered tightly in a herd, using each other's bodies to buffer themselves against the wind. I can see Jotun at the very far edge, standing by his mares. While the others rest, he's got his head raised up high, guarding them all against danger while they eat. He's always watchful, my horse – it's one of the things I love about him.

"Jotun!" I call his name and he turns to look at me. And then I whistle, and his body tenses in response. He knows what the whistle means and he whinnies back, head raised high as he calls to me. In an instant he's in flight, galloping across the long grass, coming to me. I watch his fire-mane flow out in the wind, and feel my heart soar. He's the most precious thing in the world to me.

He draws to a halt right in front of me, snorting and pawing the ground. He has a strange way of greeting me. Most Icelandic horses are cold and aloof, but not

Jotun. First, he will shove me with his muzzle, as if to say, "Hello, I'm here." And then comes the game. He will look at me sideways out of one eye and I will look at him and then our foreheads will meet and he will duck one way and then the other, and I will race to meet him, as if we're playing peek-a-boo, like a mother and baby might do. The game goes on until one of us tires of it and admits defeat – usually it's him who gives in, and instead of ducking and weaving he'll thrust his muzzle suddenly into my cheek and kiss me. His soft velvet lips will wiggle against my skin, tickling me until I collapse in giggles. Sometimes when I'm giggling he'll lick me too, almost like a dog might do. Steen says it's revolting the way he drools all over me, but he's just jealous. No one loves Steen the way Jotun loves me.

"I can't stay and play," I tell my horse. "I'm on my way to the feast. I think Father is making the announcement tonight."

Jotun stamps his hoof in the way a toddler might stamp a foot, registering his objection to me leaving again so soon.

"Jotun!" I am firm with him. "This could be big news. For both of us. Don't be childish!"

He gives his mane a defiant shake, as if he understands. Then he gives me one more smooch on the cheek, as though he's making it his decision for us to part. Flicking his head up, he turns and trots off back to the herd.

"Tomorrow," I call after him. "We'll ride then. I promise."

The feast for the chieftains is being held on the heathered plains that lie below the sacred Law Rock. Here, where the ground is flat and open, layers of goatskins have been laid down, with pillows too for the warriors to recline in comfort while the speeches on the rock take place and the feast is prepared.

For my father and the other chiefs there's a table set up front at the foot of the rock so they may sit above the rest and then stand up and speak. My father is there already when I arrive, laughing loudly with the other chiefs, holding their attention with his sagas. He knows how to tell a story of honour and strength that these men admire. He tells them of his conquests, the voyages to new lands, and the raids which bring the riches home.

The stories are always the same – voyages of slashing and killing, followed by pillaging and looting. The men lap it up as if they've never heard these tales before.

I sit on the goatskins spread at the foot of his table along with Steen and the other young warriors of our tribe, listening too. I wonder why we never hear more about the other peoples and the beauty of these strange lands – all these people my father put to the sword before we could even exchange words with them. What might have happened if he had sat down at a table like this one and met with them instead? Might we have been able to work alongside them? Trading and sharing instead of killing them outright?

These are my thoughts but they are not my words. I'm not a fool. I didn't get to be fourteen years old and still alive by speaking my mind. Instead, I laugh and I smile and I watch how my father's chieftains fawn over him in subtle ways. This is the world I live in, and I cannot change it. Not yet, anyway.

We all know why we're here, but my father wisely waits a little longer until all the men have drunk what they wish and have food in their bellies, so they are satisfied before he gets to his feet and speaks.

"For twenty years now, since I became chief of all the

tribes, we have gathered here at the sacred rock for the All-Thing," he says. "A long time..."

He shakes his head in wonder. "And now, look at me! I'm an old man."

There's a murmur of dissent. A few men even cry out: "You're still young, Lief! Not old at all!"

"No, no." My father raises a hand. "Don't flatter me. I'm ancient and I know it. And I am tired. My body aches and this crown, you see, it sits heavy on my head."

My father's power has always been in his modesty and his crown is a simple one – a gold band crafted into a point above his forehead. He reaches up now and lifts the band, placing the crown on the table in front of him.

"I have decided that, while I'm still fit and able, it's time to appoint my successor," my father says, "the one who will rule in my place after me when I'm gone."

My father holds the whole of Thing-Vellir in silence. No one dares to even breathe as they wait to hear who will take the throne.

I look at my brother Steen but he doesn't seem to notice me. He's got his eyes glued to that crown!

"And so I see that you all look to me now to hear my announcement of who will rule – but I say that it's not for me to choose the next king. This is a matter for the gods to decide," my father says. "And so, in Odin's honour, we will test the bravest and strongest and boldest of our youth in the Holmgang – a battle between rivals according to the ancient rules, as is traditional on the island in the lake at Thing-Vellir. Let the victor be the one who raises their supporters and rises up to take my crown."

I look across at my brother and see the hurt and anger on his face. He'd assumed the crown would just be passed to him with no contest. He doesn't join the others as they cheer and raise their glasses and cry out my father's name. My heart is pounding so hard the blood pulses in my ears. A Holmgang has been called! I want desperately to know the details as my father speaks on but I can't hear what he's saying now because my vision has begun to turn blurred at the edges. As he speaks, I'm gazing deep into the fire pit. The low-burning embers are stoked into life once more and bundles of rowan-tree twigs are piled on top to catch alight. I see the flames begin to lick upwards into the pale night sky, and I'm caught in their flickering glow, transported out of my own body, taken away like a wisp of smoke above the fire. I rise up and into the flames, where a girl, blonde like me, dark brows and blue eyes like my own, stares back at me and smiles. The world fades away and into her I am gone.

CHAPTER 5

Bru and Me

I re-entered my body as if I were a firework rushing out of control and crashing headlong into the ground. And there I was, suddenly sprawled on the tussock grass, panting and heaving, not knowing which way was up.

"Hilly?" It was Gudrun calling me back into myself, saying my name as she crouched down over me. How long had she been there like this? How long had I been here?

I sat up, gasping to get the air back in my lungs.

"What happened?" Gudrun was right up in my face now. "Hilly? Did you find her? What was she like? Tell me!"

I pushed her off me and leapt to my feet.

"Get away from me!" I screamed. "What did you do to me? You're a crazy woman!"

Gudrun looked taken aback. "Hilly, you need to calm down."

"Calm down? One minute I'm here and the next I'm in some Norse nightmare. I think this is about as calm as I'm going to get right now!"

There was a look of total shock on Gudrun's face. "Then it worked? You went back? You were with the Vikings?" she asked.

I nodded, speechless, only just beginning to take it in myself.

"Hilly, you know what I need to know. Tell me. Did you meet *her*?"

Gudrun's voice was soft, almost pleading. I stared into her green eyes and saw the flames rise in them.

"No, I didn't meet her," I said. "I became her."

"It was at Harvard that I first discovered how to access the true power of the ritual of the Jonsmessa." Gudrun began her story. She had wrapped me in a goatskin and I was warming myself on the dying embers of the brazier, still angry and shaken, but willing to listen. I wanted to know what had just happened to me, and Gudrun was the only one who could tell me.

"I'd just been appointed as the head of Icelandic Studies," Gudrun continued. "I knew it was an amazing opportunity as an academic – a chance to spend all my time focused on decoding the mysteries of the sagas, and working with the ancient Norse texts.

"My office was in an old brick building in the furthest wing of the Classics department on the second floor. It was very traditional, exactly like the rooms that you might imagine, with wood panelling, and stained-glass windows that looked out onto the leaves of the oak tree in the courtyard below, and a spiral staircase that led to a turret room which housed my private library. The books in there had been amassed over the years by the professors who came before me and the room contained the most important texts on Norse saga in the world. But those professors had all been men, and they were dry intellectuals. They didn't practise the rituals like I did, nor did they believe in the power of the runes, so they didn't recognise how precious the volumes on the dusty shelves of that library really were."

Gudrun sighed. "They thought the Jonsmessa was

merely a seasonal harvest festival. Bury the cow horn on the longest day of the year and watch the crops grow – that kind of thing. But I knew it was more than that. The Norse people called it the Cross-Over and the more I read about it, the more I was certain it was real – that if you did the sacred rituals absolutely right you could create a connection that would shift your body to take a different form, even transport you off this temporal plane and take you back in time. The details were all there in the books. I had studied them, figured out how to perform the rituals. I had everything I needed – except the opportunity. And then Katherine got in touch with me about this movie and she mentioned that you were coming with your mum and I knew that this was my chance."

"But why me?" I asked. "Why didn't you just send yourself back instead of dragging me into it?"

"Don't you think I wanted to go myself?" Gudrun said. "For a long time I tried to figure out a way to make this journey on my own. But the ritual clearly calls for a priestess *and* a shapeshifter. I needed to be the one who stayed behind to perform the magics. If I was trying to reach Brunhilda, then the one to cross over had to be someone about her age… someone who could connect with her."

I gave a hollow laugh. "And so you chose me? Yeah, I'm a really good match for a Norse warrior!"

"But you are, Hilly!" Gudrun locked her green eyes onto mine. "You don't see yourself clearly, not yet. But I saw something special in you as soon as we met. No one at your age can understand their potential. I was the same – I thought I was just a girl. But one day you'll realise you have something special too, and you'll see what I see in you."

"So you thought you'd just throw me into the ritual and explain it later?" I said.

Gudrun sighed. "Can you see how ridiculous it all sounds? If I had told you at the beginning what I was planning, you would never have believed me. You would have dismissed me as the rest of them do, the dancing madwoman with the burning sage. Besides, I didn't even know for sure it would work. Hilly, you say you became her? Will you at least tell me what happened?"

I snatched my hand away. It still felt strange to be back in my own body; a part of me was still *her*. I felt her wildness, her primitive nature inside of me. It was like my blood was pumping harder, my instincts were quickened. I could still feel the sense of power I'd had at that moment when my sword was pointed into the soft groove of Steen's throat. I looked at Gudrun and saw the desperation in her wide green eyes.

"I want you to know that I'm not doing this for you," I told her, "I'm telling you because that's what Brunhilda would have wanted. We have to make sure that people find out what she was really like… that they know the truth about her. I can hear what's being scripted and it isn't accurate."

"Yes." Gudrun nodded. "That's what I want too, Hilly, I promise."

And so I started Brunhilda's saga right where I came in, in the heat and noise of the arena with the stallion fight about to begin.

Gudrun and I ended up talking all night. She had so many questions – about the All-Thing, and the feasting and Brunhilda's rivalry with Steen.

"Steen shouldn't rule," I told Gudrun. "He's so selfish. Also, he's a bully. He's always pushing Brunhilda around."

I told Gudrun more about Brunhilda's horse, Jotun.

"In ancient Norse, the word translates as 'giant'," Gudrun said.

"He's huge," I confirmed. "He must be the biggest Icelandic horse I've ever seen."

Compare the magnificent Jotun to soft, delicate Troy and the chestnut stallion would look like a miniature pony beside him.

"Could Troy be made to look more like him?" Gudrun asked. "What if they dyed his coat darker?"

I shook my head. "The mane is the problem. Even if we dyed his body dark brown, Jotun's mane isn't chestnut – it's luminous, like flames."

"I'll talk to Katherine about whether we can recast the horse," Gudrun promised, "but at this late stage, we've got to be realistic. There just might not be enough time."

Time. It was a concept that had lost all meaning since I had come here. I still wasn't sleeping. That morning, after we'd done the Jonsmessa, I'd gone back to the hotel. It was already mid-morning so I'd missed breakfast. And so, exhausted by my out-of-body experience, hungry, unwashed and sleep-deprived, I headed to the stables. And in that bedraggled state, I met Anders Mortenson…

I didn't even know it was him at first. He looked like one of the crew – the usual uniform of puffer jacket, black skinny jeans and snow boots. He was bent over beside Ollie, picking out his hooves. I figured he must be one of Connor's horse-wrangling team, he had such an easy way with the stallion. Then he stood up and I was struck by how good-looking he was all at once – cheekbones that could cut glass and a ridiculously perfect white smile. His eyes were the same colour as that blue lagoon we'd swum in. His hair, naturally dark brown, had been bleached Viking-blond for the role of Prince Sigard, and with one of his hands, which were also ridiculously beautiful, elegant with tapered fingers, almost poetic, he pushed his long fringe back out of his eyes.

"Hey, you must be Hilly?"

He knew my name.

"I'm Anders," he shook my hand, very formal. "Niamh said you'd be down here this morning to exercise the horses. She's had to make a trip into

Reykjavik. She said I could ride out with you on Ollie, and that you'd ride Troy, if that's OK?"

He gave Ollie a pat and then draped an arm casually around the stallion's neck. "I figure if this guy and me are going to be working together, then we should get to know each other a bit better, right?"

I should've said, "Yes, Anders, that would be great." I should've said, "I'd love to ride with you." But I didn't because I was so aware of what a frightmare I looked at that moment, sleepless and scruffy, standing there beside him. I wasn't thinking straight.

"Why don't you get Jamisen to go with you?"

Wait a minute! My brain recoiled against my words. *You want to ride with him! Could you have sounded any less interested if you'd tried?*

"Jam's in back-to-back sessions with dialogue coaches and sword-fighting training today," Anders replied, bailing me out. "So, I'm sorry, it looks like you get the short straw."

"I'm not… I don't… You're not short," I said. D'oh. How much more stupid could I fit into one conversation?

"OK, cool, let's ride then."

Maybe Anders, who'd been a celebrity since he was ten, was used to people becoming gibbering, rude idiots in his presence or maybe he was just the world's nicest guy, but he carried on ignoring it every time I said dumb stuff and instead asked me loads of questions as we saddled up. So by the time we had the horses ready, I felt like he knew everything there was to know about me and my family – who I was and where I was from.

"New Zealand, huh?" he said. "Always wanted to go there myself. *Lord of the Rings*, that was a great movie. Looks like good horse riding country too."

Straight away it was clear Anders really did know his way around a horse. He handled Ollie with such ease as he saddled him and, when he mounted, he vaulted up on board like an Olympic gymnast, springing off his stirrup in a way that was pretty cool. I'd never in my life seen someone who looked so instantly at home on a horse.

He had his leathers so long it was like he rode with his legs almost straight, I had mine tucked up like a jockey in comparison.

"You sit like a Western rider," I observed.

"You got me," Anders said, looping his arm through the reins and holding up his hands in mock surrender. "I rode Western back home in Montana when I was growing up, but I've trained English-style too. I spent a couple of seasons showjumping when we moved to New York State, so I can do either."

The way he said "when I was growing up" made it sound like he was, like, in his thirties or something, when in fact he was only a couple of years older than me.

I know I talk a lot about how wrong Troy was to play the part of Jotun, but he was still a lovely horse – soft and gentle, a really perfect ride – and I was enjoying myself in the saddle as I rode side by side with Anders along the gravel path that wound down towards the river.

"There are flat plains with good roads along this way, good for tölt practice," I explained.

I'd only ridden at a tölt a few times myself and I was just getting the hang of how weird it felt.

"So explain this tölt thing. It's like a trot but you don't rise?" Anders asked.

"It's more like a walk-canter than a trot," I said. "It's hard to explain until you've done it. You just sit deep and keep the contact with your hands and your horse will move into it. It just comes naturally to them. That's it! Just push him on. You've got it!"

Anders really could ride. I watched him steady Ollie

back on his hocks and then, with a flick of the whip behind his leg, he pushed him forward. The black stallion surged away, in full tölt.

"Those Vikings had it sorted," he laughed. "That was so smooth, you could ride like it forever."

I showed him Ollie's tricks after that – how to make him rear with a tap of the whip behind his leg, how to get him to drop into a bow with a touch on the shoulder and how to make him lie down on his side by clucking to him as you stroked his neck.

"If I hadn't become an actor," Anders said as we rode back with the horses on the buckle, letting them walk to cool down, "I would have wanted to be a trainer, you know? I'd love to spend my days working with horses."

"You could still do it," I offered.

"Nah," Anders laughed. "I get paid too much money to be in front of the camera. I'm a spoilt Hollywood brat so now there's no going back."

"You're not a Hollywood brat," I said, kind of ignoring his obvious irony.

"Oh, I used to be," Anders replied. "You're lucky you didn't meet me when I was twelve and going through my wild years!"

I didn't know whether to believe him or not. He had a really quirky sense of humour.

"Well, you should ride your own stunts in the movie anyway," I said. "Then you and Jam could train together."

"Jam's riding her own stunts?"

I saw the look on Anders' face.

"You didn't know?"

Anders shook his head. "I heard she was getting riding lessons for the role, but that's pretty..." He hesitated, "...amazing..." He let the thought trail off, like he wasn't convinced.

"You've worked with her before then?" I asked.

"I had a guest role in her TV series as her boyfriend," Anders said. "I only appeared for one episode. I had to deliver this super cheesy line. I can still remember it."

"What was it?"

Anders suddenly changed in front of me. His glacier eyes met mine with such intensity I found myself mesmerised by the way that a crest of blond hair fell just so, allowing him a few perfect strands to gaze up through, and by that dreamy expression as he said, "Do you believe in love at first sight? Because I think I do... I think I love you."

I felt my heart slam in my chest like I'd been given an electric shock. I couldn't breathe.

"Yeah, yeah, I know, lame, huh?" Anders was all of a sudden himself again, that dreamy look replaced by his normal face.

I could see now how he'd got the role of Prince Sigard. I would have given pretty much anything to hear him say that line to me again.

That afternoon, there was a note for me pinned on the door of our cabin when I got back. It was from Gudrun and I wasn't entirely sure what it meant.

"I've found him," it said. "Come and meet me in the library as soon as you're back."

The library was a small, booklined hideaway tucked in beside the dining room in the hotel. Gudrun was there waiting for me at one of the low backgammon tables, her burgundy velvet pouch filled with runes. She had scattered the bones in front of her and was interpreting them in the same way that most people might read the paper.

"Ah, Hilly, good, you are here then!" She didn't even

look up, intent on her runes. "Do you have your warm coat with you? If not, we will need to go past your cabin and grab it before we leave."

"Leave? Where are we going?"

"North," Gudrun said. "A little village called Hovol. It's not very far. They are waiting for us there. But get a coat because it will be cold tonight."

"They?"

"The people with the horse, of course, Hilly! That is what you have come to see me about, yes? I've found the perfect horse for the film."

She swept the runes back into the velvet pouch with her left hand and pulled the drawstring tight. "I have the trailer attached. We can bring him back tonight."

"Who is he?" I said.

"He is Mjölnir," Gudrun said, "and he is the hammer of Thor."

Hovol was not really a village as much as a gathering of a dozen or so houses. We whipped through the main street so fast that Gudrun almost missed the turn-off. The stereo was on very loud, blaring out Icelandic folk music that sounded a bit like Scottish bagpipes, which was what I told her.

"It's a langspil," she said. "It has strings. Not like bagpipes at all."

"It sounds like someone's torturing a cat," I said.

Gudrun didn't turn it down despite my complaints. She was driving very swiftly considering that the roads were covered in black ice and we had a horse trailer attached to the back of the car. When at last she turned between two large wooden gates and we hit gravel roads, even then she hardly slowed, the car and trailer bumping and rocking along as we headed towards the farmhouse in the distance.

"The people here are horse breeders," Gudrun said. "The farm's been in the family for many centuries, and they're renowned for their silver dapples."

I frowned. "Jotun isn't silver at all – he's chocolate with a red mane."

Gudrun nodded. "Yes. Silver dapple is not how it sounds. These horses, they are dark brown as you say, chocolate coloured. Their manes are usually flaxen blonde, but in some cases, very unusual cases, the foal is born with a fair mane and then as it grows up the mane tints to deep red until it can become almost fluorescent, like it's on fire. They're very rare, these fire-maned horses. When you told me about Jotun, I thought a stallion of such colour and size would be very hard to find. And then I threw the runes and they told me all that I needed to know…" She pulled the car to a stop and turned the engine off, reaching over to the back seat to grab her sheepskin coat. "We're here."

There was only the farmhouse, no other buildings.

"They don't have any stables?"

Gudrun shook her head. "An Icelandic horse is tough. It doesn't need to be indoors. Even the newborn foals live outdoors without rugs. This is how they've been bred for centuries. The blood of the Viking breed, born to a life of snow and ice."

It was cold here. I stood in the driveway shivering, despite my coat and gloves. The front door to the farmhouse opened and in the light I could see a man so short he could have been a child except for his thick bushy beard. He peered out at us and shouted something in a language I didn't understand.

"That's Lars," Gudrun said. "You wait here. I won't be long."

Her tramping boots made a *crunch-crunch* on the gravel

driveway as she walked over to the house. I saw her illuminated by the light from inside and heard them speaking, in Icelandic, I guessed. Then the door closed and Gudrun returned, her boots crunching gravel once more as she swept past me towards the fields.

"Come, Hilly, this way."

Do you believe in love at first sight?

I was thinking about this as we walked. When Anders had said the words my heart had leapt, I knew that. And yes, maybe I'd got a crush on him – I mean, who wouldn't have a crush on Anders Mortenson? But it wasn't love at first sight with him – I know this because I've had love at first sight before and it was the real thing so I know how it feels.

It was three years ago when it happened to me, on a small dairy farm in Cambridge. In the car on the way there Mum had warned me that it might not work out – that you had to try out a lot of ponies before you found *the one*. This pony was a bit outside our price bracket as well, so I didn't want to get my hopes up. I remember asking what her name was and Mum said, "Piper".

I knew as soon as I saw her. I took one look at the pony standing there, and my heart was lost. I just knew in my bones that we'd be together… that she was the one. My forever pony. Until now, I'd always thought that Piper was it for me. I didn't think you were allowed more than one love-at-first-sight moment.

But when I looked out across the fields and saw the herd of horses grazing, I knew which one he was straight away and I knew, instinctively, that meeting this stallion, born of ice with a mane like fire, was the second time I would fall in love that way.

"Come," Gudrun whispered, "I want you to meet Mjölnir."

CHAPTER 6

The Hammer of Thor

On the night that we first met at that dinner in London, Gudrun had told me the story of Mjölnir…

"…how the Norse gods gave their best weapons names – and the mightiest of them all was named Mjölnir, the hammer," she began. "So powerful was Mjölnir that when Thor struck him to the ground he would make the skies thunder. When he threw Mjölnir, the hammer would always strike its target and return to his hand. And even though it was Thor alone who had the power to wield him, Mjölnir was beloved by all the gods who held him sacred as their protector. So when the hammer was stolen in the night by the ogre Thrym, the gods agreed they would do anything to get it back.

"Thrym offered them an exchange – he would return Thor's hammer for the hand in marriage of the fair goddess Freya. And the gods would have traded her too except Freya was furious and refused outright to marry a hideous ogre and so another plan was needed."

Gudrun smiled. "It was Loki, the mischievous one, who suggested that they should send Thor in Freya's place as the bride."

"I don't see how Thor could be a bride," I interrupted.

"Loki dressed him in disguise," Gudrun said. "Thor wore a long veil to conceal his red beard, and Loki accompanied him, changing shape to be his handmaiden at the bridal table. Thor took his place beside Thrym, who sat with Thor's hammer tantalisingly close, right there in his lap. The aim was to get the hammer back, but when dinner was served Thor couldn't hide his greed – he's a powerful god but he's not very bright and he's a bit of an oaf. So he gorged himself and belched loudly beneath his veil. Thrym was suspicious but Loki reassured him this was normal behaviour for a bride-to-be, and so the ogre, believing him, leaned in to his new bride for a wedding kiss, and it was then that Thor snatched the hammer back from Thrym's lap and smashed in his skull before going home quite happy with his outing, reunited with his most precious object in the universe, his hammer, his Mjölnir."

Mjölnir, not the weapon but the horse, *my very own Mjölnir*, stood before me. Very soon I would call him by his nickname and he would become Hammer. Very soon too, the bond between us would become so deep I would feel as if he were a part of me in the same way that Thor's hammer had felt as if it were an extension of the god's arm. I'd be able to call him to me too just as Thor did, shouting his name to make him return to my side. But at that first meeting, I felt as if I were in the presence of a god, because Mjölnir was the most beautiful horse I had ever seen.

He was a giant too, every bit as tall as Brunhilda's own Jotun. If anything, he was burlier, solid through the shoulders with powerful hindquarters. His stallion neck was shorter and thickened at the point of the crest so that when he caught sight of us and held his head erect he resembled more a fighting bull than a horse. At a distance he could have been Jotun – he was almost identical in colouring. As he came closer though, the differences between Hammer and Jotun became clearer. Hammer's head was more refined; every bit as noble as Jotun's, but narrower at the muzzle, with tiny, dainty ears. Beneath that fiery red forelock his eyes blazed with such a deep intensity that staring into them was almost like looking inside a volcano.

As Hammer approached, Gudrun clapped her gloved hands together in exclamation of delight. "Oh, he's magnificent!" she said. "This is a horse that is worthy of Brunhilda, yes?"

"Yes," I agreed. "He's the one."

As if he knew we were admiring him, Hammer began to arch his neck and flick up his knees, showing us the elegance of his paces. Suddenly, his stride broke and he was tölting, his knees flung high, his head held aloft as he strode out in that magical movement.

"Yes, perfect," Gudrun agreed, passing me the rope halter. "Go and fetch him while I get the horse trailer ready."

She left me there alone with this stallion tölting across the fields towards me, but I wasn't afraid. I knew he'd behave for me.

Hammer drew to a halt, his breath coming in raspy snorts, his flanks heaving. I could smell the sweetness of him, the horse-scent stronger even than the sulphur and wild heather that filled the Icelandic air. I reached out a hand for him, so that he might take in my scent too and then held my ground and let him make the first move towards me. It was almost comical the way he refused to move a hoof and managed to smell me out at a distance by stretching his neck like a giraffe. In the months that followed I would realise it was typical of him, and that all of his traits, his little quirks, would soon become so familiar to me. Though at that moment when we first met, I didn't know him at all. So when he shoved me hard with his muzzle in my back on the way to the horse trailer, I gave a squeak of surprise because I wasn't expecting it. Then I realised it was his way of showing affection and I giggled when he did it a second time. It was so quick, this shift in understanding between us. The bond formed so fast that it was almost as if, by the time we'd got him back to the Hotel Isbjörn, that we had already known each other for a lifetime.

"He's amazing," Niamh agreed when Gudrun and I brought Hammer back to the yard. Connor and Mark loved him too and the new equine star was cleared by the team, and more importantly by Katherine, to replace Troy. Niamh and Connor were so grateful to Gudrun for finding him that Connor even stopped rolling his eyes when she did crazy stuff on set, and Niamh stopped leaving the room when Gudrun joined us at breakfast, although she did complain about the smell of sage that seemed to stick to Gudrun like smoke from a fire.

If I'd had love at first sight with this horse, I think Anders felt it too.

"He's too good for Brunhilda," he said when he first saw Hammer's noble face peering out over the loose box door. "That's the sort of stallion Prince Sigard should be riding!"

I was unimpressed. "The name of the film is *Brunhilda*, remember? It's not called *Prince Sigard*."

"Yeah, yeah," Anders had teased back, "I know, but a love story needs a hero."

"She is a hero," I replied.

Gudrun had given me a copy of the most recently updated script to read, the one where she had suggested changes to Katherine based on what I'd told her from my transmogrification into Brunhilda. It was an improvement on the old script, but I still felt uncomfortable with the fairy tale ending where the helpless Princess Brunhilda, fast asleep under a magic trance, lay on a bed of stone in the centre of a burning ring of fire, waiting to be saved by the heroic Prince Sigard. The film script had it that Anders and Ollie would ride through the flames and wake her with true love's kiss. It didn't feel anything like the girl that I knew.

"How is it that a girl who was kicking her brother in the backside in a sword fight suddenly finds herself unable to wake up and needs a boy to kiss her awake?" I questioned Gudrun. "And where is Mjölnir in all of this? He'd never leave her side, even if she was in a trance. He should be with her."

"So what do you think happens to her at the end of the story then, Hilly?" Gudrun asked.

I stumbled on this question. The Cross-Over had given me a brief window into Brunhilda's world. I knew her life, I knew what she faced and I knew what she had to struggle against. I also knew how indomitable her spirit had been and sensed her determination to beat her brother Steen and take the throne. But I didn't know how it ended yet. I wasn't there.

"You need to send me back again," I said to Gudrun.
"What?"

"You did it once before," I said. "You can do it again. You're right, we still don't know her whole story, Gudrun. We need to know how she really became queen."

Gudrun's green eyes shone. "You would be willing to go back again, Hilly? It's a lot to ask of you, I know."

"I'll go back," I said. "Is there a way?"

"Yes," Gudrun said. "It is easier than you think. If you are ready, then we can do it tonight."

I would have spent the rest of the day with my belly tied in knots about it, if it weren't for the fact that I had my strangest day ever at the stables to take my mind off it. Jamisen O'Brien had finally finished her sword-fight training and dialogue coaching sessions and was at last turning up for her first meeting with Hammer.

She swept into the stable block like she was walking onto a yacht, flanked on either side by two girls who seemed about her age – which was sixteen. I would find out later they were her personal assistant, Bebe, and her make-up artist, Alyssa. The others in the group were a woman dressed in a suit and heels, carrying an enormous handbag and talking on her mobile the entire time was Jamisen's agent, Melissa, and hovering right beside Jam was an older man, heavily tattooed and shaven-headed but with a massive beard. He was wearing white jeans and a white T-shirt and looking deeply disturbed at the idea of being near the horses. He turned out to be her hairstylist, Tonney, and at his side, as muscled as a body builder, fake-tanned, wearing shorts, a crop top and shivering underneath an enormous puffer jacket, was Jamisen's personal trainer, Amanda Lansing.

In the middle of them all, surrounded like a president flanked by secret service agents, Jamisen O'Brien was blonde, blue-eyed, clear-skinned and the same height as me – I hadn't been expecting that since on TV she had always looked taller. She was about the same build as me too. I remember how our eyes met and I smiled because I had this weird feeling – like we'd been friends forever because I'd grown up watching her every night on *The Jam O'Brien Show*. But of course I didn't know her at all. And she was different here to the way she was on TV as well. Jam O'Brien on television was bright and chatty. This girl stood detached from the conversation, saying nothing as Melissa spoke intently to Niamh.

"We understand you've re-cast Jamisen's horse without her approval or consultation." Melissa still had her phone to her ear as she spoke so it was hard to tell whether she was talking to Niamh or to the person on the other end of the line. "We'd like sign-off on him, please."

Niamh looked taken aback. "I'm not sure that Jamisen has the right of approval over the horses," she said. "Anyway, Katherine has already signed off on him."

Melissa rolled her eyes. "Don't make me bounce back to Katherine on this. I want to see him now."

Niamh looked worried. "Yeah, I mean, of course. We were expecting Jamisen to ride him today anyway. We've got some stunts to run through before filming begins tomorrow."

"She won't be riding today," Melissa said. "She's got script changes to look at and back-to-back meetings."

It seemed really weird how this conversation was going on between the two women while Jamisen herself stood just a few feet away, chatting to her friends and paying no attention at all, as if it didn't involve her.

"When will she have a chance to run through them then?" Niamh said uncertainly. "The opening scene requires a galloping dismount. That's going to take some practice. We could meet back down here late this afternoon maybe?"

Melissa sighed. "We've got a Skype call with LA this afternoon. And Jam has dialogue coaching after that."

"I know she's busy –" Niamh was frustrated – "but

she needs to run through the stunts before we begin filming…"

"Mel?" Jamisen interrupted them. "Do I need to be here while you handle this? Or can I get back to the room?"

Melissa raced to her side and gave her a hug. "Of course, honey! You rest up. I've got this."

"Thanks, Mel." Jamisen looked so grateful, it was as if Melissa had just offered to solve world hunger. She double cheek-kissed her and left, with Alyssa, Bebe, Tonney and Amanda clustered protectively around her. She didn't say goodbye to us and she hadn't even cast a glance at Hammer.

Melissa waved goodbye to Jam and then turned back to Niamh. "Here's the thing," she said. "Jamisen really isn't comfortable getting on a horse in front of people."

"Wow!" Niamh absorbed this information with a deep breath. "Umm, so we seem to have very crossed wires about this. We were told Jamisen would be riding in all of the scenes and doing all her own stunts. That's what we've been prepping for."

"I hear what you're saying," Melissa said. "Unfortunately, in her contract Jamisen is only committed to do close-up shots with the horse on a closed set. So you'll need to work around her needs."

"Only close-ups? She won't ride at all? Seriously?" Niamh shook her head in disbelief. "You mean to tell us that Katherine has cast an actress who won't ride when we're shooting the first horseback scenes tomorrow?"

Melissa didn't look at all fazed by Niamh's outburst. "I hear what you're saying," she said once more, "so maybe you should get your stunt double down to the costume department for a wig fitting. She's going to be on camera – a lot."

Melissa's high heels made an emphatic *click-clack* as she strode back out of the stables in Jamisen's wake, leaving Niamh and me with the horses in desperate silence.

"Find a stunt double? Yeah, right..." Niamh said. She looked at me, eyeing up my height, my physique, and in that instant I knew what she was thinking before she even said the words: "Go and get fitted for a wig."

When I met Gudrun in the library that evening, I was feeling overwhelmed.

"I know this seems a lot to take on, but really it could

be for the best," Gudrun said. "You already have a bond with Hammer, which will translate on the screen."

"But I'm not an actor." I felt sick at the prospect of being on set tomorrow with everyone staring at me.

"Jamisen will still do the close-ups," Gudrun said. "They'll never even see your face." She edged closer to me, her voice soft now so that no one could overhear us. "Going back to what we talked about this morning – I think it's very brave of you to offer to go back again, to find out more. Is that still what you want? Are you certain?"

I nodded. "Yes."

"Very good," Gudrun said. "So shall we do it right now?"

"Now?"

"If you're ready, yes. Why not?" Gudrun said.

I'd imagined that we'd have to go back to the Colosseum… that the rituals would need to be repeated, the cow horn buried and dug up again.

"All we need is the necklace," Gudrun explained. "Are you wearing it?"

I was.

"Then come over by the fire with me."

106

The library of the hotel was totally quiet at that time of night. The polar bear looked almost lonely standing there in the corner on his hind legs, jaws open and paws outstretched. Gudrun led me past him and we took our places in the two overstuffed armchairs on either side of the fireplace, where an open fire was crackling away, flames licking up the chimney.

"On the night of the Jonsmessa, you remember how you looked into the flames to be transported?" Gudrun said. "Do it again now, Hilly. Look at the flames and allow yourself to move within them."

I did as she said, gazing into the fireplace. It was fascinating the way the flames moved when you stared at them hard. Some were constant, licking up into the air and then receding but always in the same place. Others moved much faster than the rest, peaking and disappearing, only to reappear somewhere else, shifting shape, changing form. It was these flames that I became absorbed by as I sat there. I watched the shape-changers as they came alive and disappeared again before my eyes and, as they mesmerised me, I felt myself move inside them, until I wasn't there any more. And once again, I was slipping away, until I became *her.*

CHAPTER 7

The Island

Last night I sat at the fireside and I threw the runes. I read them and I saw that Odin would take my side against Steen, his black ravens, Thought and Memory, on his shoulders to advise me. His wisdom will be my power. This battle will be a test of intellect and my dimwitted brother Steen walks into it unarmed.

"Steen's not fit to rule," my friend Hannecke says as she rides her mare, Mari, alongside me and Jotun. "You must challenge him and take your rightful place as queen."

I clasp her hand in my own and clutch it to my breast, holding her there in confirmation of our sisterhood.

"Thank you, Hannecke," I say. "What about the others? Are they with us?"

For the past week, Hannecke and I have held secret meetings with the young people of our tribe. Since it was impossible to gather in my longhouse, for fear of alerting Steen, we met at Hannecke's instead and sometimes at our other friend Astrid's. Everyone was welcome and all voices have been heard. When it was my turn to speak, I told them quite plainly that I had brought them together because I wanted to defeat my brother and be queen because I would be the better ruler for our tribe. A few of the boys resisted even talking about this at first. Erik said he thought it was wrong for a woman to rule him and that should be the end of the matter.

"A man should be in control, it's the natural order," he insisted.

"But you saw how Bru got the better of Steen in the sword fight," Hannecke pointed out to him. "She's the better warrior."

"She got lucky!" Kari countered.

I raised my hand to stop them quarrelling. "That fight was a duel with blunt swords," I said. "In battle against our enemies with real weapons, there are lives at stake. In the midst of the bloodlust and frenzy, split-second decisions need to be made. So I ask you, who would you rather have leading you at that moment?"

I looked pointedly at Kari. "You want to be led by a bully king who rules you with fear and intimidation? Who thinks of nothing but himself and killing for the spoils? Who can use only a sword and not his head? Or would you rather have a lion-hearted leader who will open up dialogue with new worlds and take you on adventures as her equal, treating you with fairness and respect? I may be a girl but I have the heart of a king. You have seen the runes. Odin is on my side. It is time for change."

Long ago I watched my father speak at the All-Thing and I realised then that the power of his kingship lay not in his fists, but in his voice. I knew my speech had won them over that night. Even Erik.

"All of them seem converted... all of them except Kari," Hannecke tells me. "I don't know why he's loyal to Steen when Steen is so horrible to him."

"He's weak-minded," I say. "And Liesl will side with them too. Poor Liesl thinks she's in love with Steen. I think she believes he will marry her and she'll become a queen."

Hannecke rolls her eyes. "So they are on his side. And

perhaps Steen will convince Frey and Alf, two others from our tribe, to fight for him too, because they'll do anything if you pay them enough money. So Steen has the numbers he needs to challenge for the crown. He'll have to take three of his supporters to the island to fight with him. The rest of us will all commit our allegiance to you. You can choose who you want from our ranks – the best three warriors to even the numbers against him – and we will fight at your side."

The battle lines between myself and Steen have divided our tribe.

Once we win though, I'm certain it will be easy to restore unity. Steen's "friends" are fickle and will desert him without a second thought. Bullies like Steen can swell their ranks briefly, but they never earn lifelong loyalty because their reign relies on intimidation.

I'm lucky to have Hannecke as my right-hand woman. She's a good warrior with great instincts and, as we ride for Thing-Vellir together, we discuss the merits of our team – how to put together the ultimate group of four fighters, the strengths and weaknesses of each member weighing against the others. Hannecke will fight at my side. Yes, I have chosen her because she's my friend and she's loyal, but I have also chosen her because she's swift with an axe and can throw her weapon almost as well as she can use it in hand-to-hand combat. The two boys to join us will be Erik and Finn.

"They are old friends of Steen's and this works in our favour," I tell Hannecke. "They've fought often with him and know how he thinks."

"Finn is clever and Erik is strong," Hannecke agrees. "Erik's muscles will come in useful if the combat turns to open hand."

There's no need to kill to win this contest. A surrender is all that's required, but it will not be easy.

"Steen will fight to the bitter end," I tell Hannecke. "It won't be over for certain this time until my sword is once again in the soft groove of his throat and he has taken the knee to me as his queen."

It feels strange to be back at Thing-Vellir so soon after the celebrations. We set up camp and, as we lay down goatskins and pitch sticks to construct makeshift shelters for the night, I think about what Steen said about my own wedding being next.

"I overheard the men planning it," Hannecke tells me. "They say that Prince Sigard from Greenland has been put forward by his own father as your suitor and that your father approves the union."

I am fourteen and already they are marrying me off to a boy I don't even know. How dare they decide my fate for me! When I beat Steen tomorrow and become the queen regent, then I will state a new law that women may choose their own destiny and their own husband – if they choose to marry at all.

"I don't like the sound of this Sigard," I tell Jotun when I go to say goodnight. "I don't need a husband."

Jotun is grazing happily with his herd tonight but he's been having problems of his own with pretenders to his throne. When you're the lead stallion, there's always a usurper in the ranks trying to work his way up. None of the other colts have ever succeeded. He's too massive, too mighty and too powerful to be beaten by another horse. His body is scarred with battle wounds from seeing off opponents. Patches of white hair grow against his dark coat where the wounds never healed quite cleanly on his shoulder and his rump. He's the best fighting stallion in Iceland, my horse. All the same, I worry about him being hurt. One day there will be a colt who overthrows him. That's how it is when you are the king.

The Holmgang on the island tomorrow is a serious business – not like my last fight with Steen. We won't be using blunted swords. The weapons will be real. I could die. I'm trying not to think about the fact that this might be the last time I ever see Jotun.

If I'm killed in the battle, then I won't be here to protect my horse. Steen will take him as his own and that thought is so awful I cannot even contemplate it.

"If that happens, then you must run," I tell Jotun. "Better you live out your life as a wild creature than be shackled to Steen's cruelty, do you understand me?"

I hug him goodnight, but when I try to let go, Jotun hooks my shoulder into the crook of his jaw so that I'm trapped in his embrace.

"Jotun!" I squirm. "It's bedtime. Let me go!"

But he doesn't release me.

"OK," I sigh. "There's no reason for me to return to camp, I suppose. I can sleep the night out here with you."

I throw down a goatskin and wrap myself in fox pelts, curling up in a ball at his feet. Jotun lowers his muzzle to sniff my cheek. When he sees that I'm planning to sleep, he gives a satisfied grunt and drops to his knees beside me. Then he rolls down onto his side to make room for me so I can snuggle closer between the crook of his forelegs with my head on his belly.

It's almost dawn when I open my eyes again. The whole valley of Thing-Vellir is shrouded in thick fog. I leave Jotun to sleep.

"I won't speak of goodbyes," I whisper to him. And no more thoughts of defeat or death. I'm done with that. I'm determined to return to reclaim my horse.

I walk alone through the mist, following the natural chasm between the rock cliffs, away from the sacred rock going down towards the sea-lake. People are gathered already on the foreshore and I see that Steen is there before me. He's dressed in chain mail and a helmet. At his side, as we predicted, Kari and Frey stand with him. But not Liesl. I knew she wouldn't be allowed to join him – my brother would never think of including a girl in a fight. Instead, he has chosen Alf to join his ranks. It's what I expected of him and I'm pleased. Liesl is actually half-decent with a crossbow – I've hunted with her many times and she can kill a squirrel in a tree at fifty paces. Alf, on the other hand, has never been very dangerous with any weapon that I've ever seen him wield.

When Steen sees that I've chosen Erik and Finn to fight with me, my brother's face turns very dark. And in that moment I know we already have the advantage. An angry warrior or a scared one amounts to the same thing. Emotions render them useless. I don't have emotions when I fight.

"My son Steen has laid his claim to the crown," my father says. "Is there another who will stand against him?"

For a moment there's silence. Behind me I feel Hannecke give me a sharp dig in the ribs. I turn to look at her and smile. I know what I'm doing. I am playing with Steen, letting him get a quick rush of blood at the idea he might pluck the crown unchallenged. And then I step forward.

"I will stand, Father."

"Brunhilda." My father cocks an eyebrow. "You challenge your own brother?"

"Somebody needs to," I reply.

There's a titter of laughter from our group.

Steen looks furious.

"You're not a man's equal and not a man at heart," he says.

It is the traditional taunt of the Holmgang.

And I reply in the traditional way too: "I am as much a man as you."

There are two longboats waiting for us on the foreshore. I lead my team on board the one on the left-hand side and walk to the bow. My father's men push the boats into the lake and take up the oars to row us out. The island isn't far. There's just a narrow channel of water to cross to reach it from Thing-Vellir – we could swim if we needed to, except the water is icy cold.

This island is where all Holmgangs are settled. Once we're on the island, the fight begins. We won't leave until one of us has won.

I've never been here before and, as the longboat approaches, I examine the terrain. The island is dense with trees, forested to the far north, and then it turns barren with windswept tussock grass in the south. There's no beach – it's steep on all sides with rocky cliffs down to the sea. Our longboats won't be able to land here. They'll just pull in close enough for us to leap overboard and swim the final distance.

In the tussock field, the scene has been set for the battle. On top of the tussock grass, a leather hide has been stretched and pegged to the ground. On the hide they've laid the weapons we may use against each other. Whoever reaches the Holmgang first may choose their instruments of war, so it's vital that as many of us as possible make it there before Steen's gang can claim them.

Seven boat lengths from the cliffs, the men cease rowing. My father, who stands beside Steen at the prow, says something to my brother that I cannot hear. Does he want Steen to win? I've always thought I was his favourite child but Steen is the son, and higher in my father's eyes perhaps, despite the fact that he's dumb and cruel.

My father makes his men hold their boats steady with the oars as I move forward to the prow with Hannecke, Finn and Erik at my side. We perch ourselves on the boat's edge as the waves threaten to topple us off and wait for my father to raise the cow horn to his lips and signal us. It's carved with runes, bone bleached white. He holds it high to the sky and speaks a prayer to Odin and then he takes a deep breath and sounds the bellow that begins the Holmgang.

118

I leap headfirst. While the others are still scrabbling over the side, I'm in the water and stroking hard, swimming with the swell, heading for the rocks. When I feel my hands scrape the jagged sea floor on the downstroke I stop swimming and stand up in waist-deep water. Quickly, I begin to clamber over the rocks.

I fall into the water and plant my hands in front of me, stumbling and rising, swamped by waves. Pushing myself up, I tumble again and then I'm out of the water at last and clawing my way with raw fingers up the steep cliff face. Beside me, Hannecke is almost as swift and determined as I am. Both of us are out in front of the others. I don't look back but I know that Steen will be right there chasing us down.

I crawl up the cliff like a spider. My hands are aching and bleeding from gripping tree roots and rocks, and when at last I reach the top, I throw myself down on the tussock grass, heaving great gulps back into my lungs. No time to recover! Pushing myself up to my feet again, my wet trousers cling to me, soggy boots and chain mail slowing me down. I'm still quick, even in these heavy clothes and beside me Hannecke is quicker still. She was always a magnificent runner and now she's out in front of me, first to reach the ground where the animal hide is stretched and pick up her weapons.

The rules of the Holmgang are simple – you can choose as many weapons as you can carry. Hannecke's weapons of choice are both axes – one long-handled and one short – and two shields. I'm right behind her, grabbing up the crossbow and a short sword. I too take two shields for protection. I consider a second axe but I know it will weigh me down too much to run and Steen must be right behind us. I'm not ready to face him yet.

"Take cover!" I tell Hannecke. "Get into the trees!"

And now I am running again, my feet sloshing in my wet boots, crossbow strapped to my back, the shields bouncing against each other across my shoulder. I hope Erik and Finn will make it in time to grab swords for themselves too – in close combat they are both good swordsmen.

Keep running, keep moving, because right now the most important part of our strategy is to put as much distance as possible between us and the Holmgang zone. The further we can get into the forest, the greater our advantage.

So I run. I run until my legs ache and my chest is about to burst. The weight of the sword in my hand and the shields on my shoulder make me stumble as I vault over fallen logs and duck beneath the boughs of trees. I'm deep in the forest when, behind me, I hear the crashing of footsteps through the undergrowth, and then there's the sound of someone breathing hard at my back. I turn and pull my sword, ready to fight.

"Bru, no!" I lower my weapon. It's Finn. He's holding a sword and strapped to his back is a double-headed short axe. He's done well.

"Finn!" I hug him. "Did you see Erik?" I ask. "Is he safe? What did he get?"

But before Finn can answer me, I hear the swish of an arrow leaving a bow, and then, in front of my eyes, Finn gasps and slumps forward, hands gripping his belly.

"Finn!" I pull his hands away to see what has struck him. There's the barbed point of an arrow penetrating his belly.

"Finn!"

He collapses forwards onto me, gasping in shock.

"Bru?" Finn's face is white, as if he can't believe he's really been shot.

"It's OK, hang on to me. I've got you." I grab him and tuck myself under his shoulder to hold him upright as I put my shield up in the direction the arrow came from to protect us both. Then I drag him, stumbling and lurching into the undergrowth.

"Is it bad?" Finn asks.

"No," I lie to him. The arrow has gone clean through him. I need to get it out. He won't be able to move while it's stuck inside him.

"Hold still," I instruct him. "This isn't going to hurt."

Another lie.

I grab the arrowhead that is sticking out of his bleeding stomach and with a brutal twist I snap off the shaft.

Finn winces in pain.

He is about to say something but before he can speak I grab the other end of the arrow shaft and pull hard, wrenching the arrow clean out of his body.

Finn collapses on the ground beside me, panting with pain.

"Breathe," I tell him, "just breathe. I'm going to stuff the wound on both sides with rags to stop the bleeding."

I lift up his shirt to get a look at the wound. "You're going to be OK," I say. "It was a clean shot through your side, and there's not too much blood. Try not to move. Stay low, and take my shield to hide behind. I'm going looking for whoever it was that shot you."

I grab the crossbow off my back and place an arrow from the quiver into it.

Finn is groaning with pain. "Be quiet!" I hiss softly at him. "Shove a rag in your mouth if you need to. I must listen."

I focus my thoughts and clear my head, ignoring Finn's whimpers as I tilt my head to the wind. I'm like a fox searching for prey with ears cocked. I can hear the birds in the trees above us, the squirrels racing from bough to bough. And then, to the left of me, and about twenty strides ahead of us, I hear the tiny, almost imperceptible snap of a twig. Without hesitating, I turn on the sound and lock my eyes on the target before loosing the arrow in my crossbow. There is a clean thud as it hits Kari's shield. I reload and am about to aim again, but then I see Kari is struggling to reload his bow, so instead of sending another arrow at him, I see my chance. Springing across the clearing, my sword in my hand, I lunge at him, hacking at his shield so that he drops it. Now he's defenceless on the ground, cowering with his hands over his head to protect himself.

I hold my sword up, as if I'm about to strike a killing blow and Kari whimpers.

"You surrender?"

"I do," Kari says. He's trembling, and his pants are soaking wet from leaping out of the longboat, or at least I hope that is why they are wet!

"Don't tell Steen that I gave in so easily," he begs me.

"I won't," I promise him. My brother would be brutal to Kari if he knew he'd been so quick and pathetic in defeat. He lacks honour and I feel sorry for him. A true warrior knows that we do not need to fear the fight because Odin has already chosen the method and moment of our death. The gods are always watching us and only the truly brave in battle get chosen by Odin to rise up and join him and the Aesir, the gods, at the great feast. So if you ask me, Kari should forget about Steen and worry instead about displeasing Odin. Based on his performance today, nobody is setting a place at the table in Valhalla for him anytime soon.

"You surrender, so you are one of us now," I tell him, easing him down onto the ground in front of the tree. "Take care of Finn for me. Pack his wound, build a fire to warm you both and keep him awake. I'll be back."

I slide the crossbow and axe onto my back, sheathe my sword, hook a shield onto my arm and straighten my chain mail.

"I'm going to find Hannecke and Erik," I tell Finn. "Kari will look after you until I return."

I am no longer trying to be silent as I run on through the trees. It's impossible carrying this many weapons to be light on my feet and, besides, I want them to know I'm coming. Before I left him, Kari told me that he was the only one of his team to take a bow and arrow. The others carry broadswords, axes and shields. If they come at me now it will be in face-to-face combat, not firing at a distance. So they have lost the element of surprise and I will know about it if they come into range.

"Aieee!"

A crashing through the undergrowth accompanies the battle cry from the left of me. That's the side I carry my sword. I manage to unsheathe it and spin in plenty of time to confront Alf as he bears down on me with his long axe. I hack at the axe handle, and he braces back and shoves my sword clean out of my hands. I react swiftly before he can use his advantage, flinging myself at him bare-handed with a battle roar, tackling him to the ground, making him drop his axe and then sitting on his chest as I rain my fists on him. Alf is stronger than me and he flips me onto my back. Now I am pinned beneath him and he reaches his hand over his own back to grasp his back-up weapon, which is a short axe. His hand never reaches its goal, however, because Hannecke is behind him. She takes him in a headlock and, wasting no time, unsheathes her sword to put the edge of the blade to Alf's throat.

"Surrender or die," she says.

"So there are two of them still out there," Hannecke says as we walk back to join Kari and Finn. "Steen and Frey."

"And Erik too," I say. "As far as we know."

We haven't seen Erik since we left the longboats.

Back in the clearing, we find Kari has built a fire as I told him to, and Finn is sitting up beside him. He's pale and a little shaken but I don't think that he will die. He's delighted to see we've taken Alf prisoner too.

"How soon until this is over?" he groans with his hand at his gut as we collapse down on the ground beside the fire with them. Finn's clothes are crusted with his blood but he's nearly dry from the flames. Hannecke and I are still wet and I'm feeling the cold seeping into my bones. I need to warm up and gather my thoughts.

"We rest here briefly and then head for the other end of the island where there aren't any trees," I say. "Steen's weapons are all suited to hand-to-hand combat. We need to be in an open space so we can see him coming and be ready for him."

I warm myself a little longer at the fire and then Hannecke and I rise up again and hunt for food. I shoot a squirrel with my crossbow while she gathers moss, crowberries and mushrooms, and we use my helmet to heat our foraged morsels with the scrags of squirrel meat. It's not quite a feast but it certainly heats our bellies.

We need to keep our strength up. Steen is out there with Frey on his side and I know better than to underestimate my brother. We haven't won the Holmgang yet.

"Bru?" I can hear Hannecke's voice. "Bru, we need to get moving. It's not safe here. Bru?"

My mind is wavering as I stare into the flames. Why is the world around me blurring at the edges?

"Bru?" I can hear Hannecke calling my name.

And then another voice, calling me too, pulling me

further into the flames, taking me away from her. Woodsmoke burns in my lungs as I gasp and resist.

No! Not now. Not in the middle of the Holmgang! But there is no way I can stop the flames from taking me deep into them and I hear the voice deep within the fire calling me by name.

"Hilly. Hilly..."

And I am gone.

CHAPTER 8

True Love's Kiss

I emerged from the flames like a diver breaking the water's surface, startled and gasping for air.

"Hilly?" Gudrun was holding me in her arms as I heaved and quivered. My lungs, desperate for oxygen, gulped it in.

"It's OK, Hilly, you're back," Gudrun said. "Take deep breaths, that's the way…"

I wrenched myself free from her, bending over with my hands on my knees.

"What am I doing here?" I coughed. "Why did you bring me back?"

"Because I thought I was going to lose you." Gudrun looked anxious. "Hilly, you were so deep in the trance this time I could sense you growing cold, and your pulse had slowed so that I could barely feel it. I began to fear that if you stayed like that any longer, that…"

"No! You shouldn't have! Make me go back to the island!" I insisted.

"The island?" Gudrun asked.

"At Thing-Vellir. They took her and Steen there in the longboats and left them to fight," I gasp. "They called it the Holmgang. There were two sides and Bru was fighting against Steen. Finn's in Bru's team and he's hurt and she's captured two of the others but Steen and Frey are still on the island somewhere and they'll be coming for her…"

I collapsed back into a chair. I was exhausted.

"Hilly," Gudrun said firmly, "I understand that you're worried for her, but you know you can't go back again, not yet. It's too dangerous for you to transform again now straight away. You need to rest, regather your energy."

She was right. I was wrung out, I could barely stand. I stayed where I was, slumped limp in the chair.

"What you've witnessed, this ritual of the Holmgang," Gudrun said, "it's an ancient Norse tradition, a sacred duel of honour. For many years historians have debated what form it took, what the rules were and where it took place. Hilly, you alone have seen it and know the truth. You must tell me everything…"

I nodded weakly. "They take them there on longboats," I began, "two teams of four…"

As I told Gudrun about the Holmgang that night, the fire in the library burned away to embers and then they died, too. She wanted to know it all, every little detail – the weapons chosen, the voyage to the island, the rules of the game and how you could win or lose. With every word I spoke, her green eyes brightened, almost as if she were using me, draining the last of my energy from me. I knew it wasn't really like that. It wasn't Gudrun who'd exhausted me – it was the transmogrification that had done me in. And Gudrun was right – I needed to regain my energy reserves and feel whole again before I could undertake the journey through the fire once more.

Finally, Gudrun looked at me as if she'd only just noticed how tired I was, and said, "I think it's time for bed."

I was just standing up from my chair when Niamh came into the library, looking almost more exhausted than me.

"I've been doing final run-throughs for tomorrow," she said. "Anders came down to the stables after he'd finished filming so we could go through all his stunts. He was amazing – you know, he'd already spent all day on set but he made the time to come and rehearse. We ran through all of the moves that you and I had already practised and he nailed it all. He didn't complain about how tired he was, either. He's amazing to work with. He's so not 'Hollywood', you know?"

"That's great," I said. I was so tired just standing up out of my chair I wanted to collapse, but I couldn't say that right now to Niamh. I was supposed to be stunt-riding with Anders tomorrow and I didn't want to worry her.

"Anyway," Niamh continued, "I just wanted to check you had your pink papers for tomorrow."

Pink papers were a film thing – they were the last-minute changes that had been made to the script and actors were issued them, often just the night before filming took place. I'd seen a stack of them on the kitchen table in my cabin that Lizzie had dropped off earlier.

"Yeah, I've got them but I haven't looked yet," I said.

"I didn't think I needed to read those. I'm not acting or anything, I just do stunts."

"Yes," Niamh said, "except the script changes also say what stunt scenes you'll be riding in Jamisen's place. And tomorrow they've got you in the horseback fight scene with Anders. Except now they're including the end sequence between Sigard and Brunhilda."

"They're doing what?" I was confused.

"They're filming it as part of the stunt," Niamh said. "I just wanted to make sure you knew."

"Knew what?"

"Tomorrow," Niamh said. "First scene up, you're on camera. And you have to kiss Anders Mortenson."

"I don't think I can do this."

I was in Hammer's loose box, slumped down on the straw on the floor. The stallion had his muzzle pressed up against my cheek, nuzzling me in sympathy.

I had read the pink papers last night after we had spoken and Niamh was right: Anders and I would sword fight and, at the end, we would kiss.

"And there's going to be all these people watching

me and I've never even kissed a boy in real life, let alone my first kiss being with Anders Mortenson! I can't possibly do it…"

Hammer gave me a hard nudge with his nose.

"Yeah," I said, "I know. Bru has worse problems than me. You're right. I need to keep it together. It's just a kiss, right? How hard can it be?"

I took Hammer's thick, silken forelock in my hands and split it into three before braiding it like I was plaiting him for a horse show.

"OK, so I'm doing it. But you'll have to stick with me, no matter how badly I mess it up, OK?" I whispered to him. "I need to know you've got my back, OK?"

Hammer gave a snort and shook out his mane, which made me lose the ends of the braid as it splayed apart. I picked it up again and this time he stayed still until I'd finished the plait and twirled it up into a topknot.

"There!" I said to him. "You look pretty!"

Hammer half-closed his eyes, making it clear that looking pretty was not a priority for him.

"OK, OK, I was just fooling around," I said. "You know, boy horses can wear their hair in braids too?"

Piper used to love it when I plaited her mane. All those mornings in competition season had made me really quick. I could pretty much do it blindfold, since it was usually dark when I'd get to the yard in the morning, and we'd stand there together, her and me, all alone with the eerie light of the tack room glowing out on us, just enough so I could see what I was doing.

Sometimes it felt unfaithful for me to be here with Hammer, to be braiding his mane the way I used to braid Piper's. He was so different in every way to her. Piper had this fine-boned look and was so sensitive about everything. In the winter she would wear three rugs to keep her from shivering. Hammer was the opposite. He was tough. Like Gudrun said, he'd been born into snow and ice, and his forefathers had been ridden by Vikings. And yet he could be so soft with me. I felt this connection with him, just as I had done with her. I missed her so much and yet here, in the middle of nowhere, on the other side of the world, I had found a horse that I loved just as much as I loved her. And at that moment, sitting in the stall with Hammer and unplaiting the braid from his mane, I didn't feel scared or lonely any more. I felt lucky.

Hammer gave me a nudge with his muzzle as if to say, "Are you still here?"

"Yeah, yeah," I told him, "I know. I'm going already, OK?"

I knew that I was stalling, hanging out with him here to avoid being at the make-up trailer. I was terrified. What if I blew it today? I'd never been in front of the cameras before.

"I'll just stay here a little while longer," I whispered to Hammer.

He gave another snort and this time shook his mane even more vigorously. I got the message. I left the stables and took myself off to get ready for work.

"I'm looking for Bobbi?" Nervously, I stuck my head around the door of the make-up trailer.

"Honey, you just found her!" A woman wearing a scarlet jumpsuit and braids beckoned me in. "You must be Hilly? Come in and shut the door behind you. You're letting all the cold air in!"

The make-up trailer was warm and cosy, and Bobbi had it cluttered up with stuff. Every bit of counter space was covered in make-up or old disposable coffee cups. Sketches of Vikings and pictures and drawings of runes and tattoos were pinned onto the mood board beside the mirrors.

Bobbi swept me up and deposited me in the make-up

chair and spun it round so that I was facing the mirror. "Ooh, prepare yourself for transformation, honey," she cooed, "I'm gonna turn you into a Norse goddess!"

I looked at the face staring back at me from the make-up mirror, caught sight of the sleep-deprived dark under-eye circles and wind-bitten pink cheeks.

"I don't see why I even need make-up on me," I protested. "Jamisen's the one they'll see in all the close-ups. I'm just doing stunts."

"And it's my job to make you look just like her," Bobbi said. "Even in the distance you'd be surprised how much detail the camera picks up. Now don't argue with me, you're only making it harder for yourself. Get a magazine and make yourself comfortable and let me do my job!"

I sat quietly after that, not daring to question Bobbi as she went about her work, sponging and dabbing at my face, smearing my skin with pale alabaster foundation. Base, she called it. Once that was done she took another sponge and began working in a different colour, contouring what had previously been my non-existent cheekbones. "It's all about creating an illusion, Hilly. Once we finish with you in this chair, honey, you'll *be* Brunhilda."

Yeah, well it wouldn't be the first time, I muttered under my breath.

There was a knock on the trailer door and Mum stepped inside.

"Hey there, Jillian," Bobbi said, without looking up. "She's only just got in the chair so don't even start on me if you're here to hurry me up…"

"Mind-reader!" Mum confirmed. "Bobbi, I hate to pressure you but I really need her in wardrobe."

"They didn't hurry the Sistine Chapel, honey," Bobbi said. "So don't you be trying to rush me, OK?"

Mum sighed. "I know. We're all trying to accommodate the changes to the schedule. Just be as quick as you can, OK? That's all I'm asking."

"I'll do my best, honey," Bobbi said, still with her eyes focused on the mirror and my face as she carried on dusting and powdering my skin. She waited until Mum had closed the door behind her before she gave a laugh.

"…but I ain't promising."

Bobbi gave me a final powder dust. "Done!" she said. "Now let's get that hair happening."

I have quite a lot of hair, so it took Bobbi a while to get it under the hair cap.

138

"I look bald," I said.

"Patience…" Bobbi tutted as she fussed over me. "I'm workin' magic here."

The wig sat on a styrofoam head. It was thick, flaxen blonde, and so long at the back that it fell all the way to the floor. At the front, it was swept up into a quiff at the crown with a topknot and two tiny braids, one at each temple. It was the exact same hairstyle the real Brunhilda had worn that first day at the stallion fight at the Colosseum. I'd described it afterwards for Gudrun, and she'd asked if I could draw her a picture too, and this picture was now pinned up on Bobbi's mood board right in front of me.

"Hilly," Bobbi said, "I'm gonna need your help here, honey. Hold it like that… good. Now tilt your head all the way forward."

I flipped my head forward like she told me and found myself submerged in a mass of flaxen hair. It was hard to breathe under there as Bobbi worked the wig so that it fitted perfectly all the way around my hairline at the back of my head.

"OK, it's on," Bobbi said. "You can sit up again!"

I raised my head up and instantly reeled back in shock. The girl staring back from the mirror wasn't me.

With the wig and the make-up, the transformation had taken place. I had become *her.*

I was Brunhilda.

"Beautiful," Bobbi said, looking pleased with her handiwork.

"Fabulous as always, Bob," Mum agreed when she came back in. "Don't you think so, Hilly?"

"Yes," I replied, my voice a whisper. I was still taking in the fact that I now looked just like *her.* A chill ran down my spine.

Bobbi held me by the shoulders and looked at my reflection. "Didn't I tell you I could work miracles?" She took a comb handle and poked at the wig with it, adjusting a few strands, wiggling the braids into place so that they sat perfectly.

"How does that feel?" she asked. "Go on. Give it a shake. Don't be shy!"

"It's good," I said, giving my head a vigorous nod back and forth, "it feels secure."

Bobbi spun the chair around. "All yours, Jillian," she said.

Mum stepped up and looked at me in the mirror. She peered quizzically at me.

"What's wrong?" I said.

"Nothing, sweetie," Mum said. "It's just amazing how that blonde wig makes your eyes look so blue." She smiled at me. "Or maybe I just don't recognise you because I've hardly seen you these past few weeks. I'm sorry, but you know how busy I get once I'm on location. It's been sixteen-hour days. Are you doing OK?"

"I'm good, Mum." I squeezed her hand. It was a relief to me that she felt like she'd been ignoring me rather than worrying about where I was all the time.

We walked together from the make-up trailer to the costume room with Mum talking to Lizzie on her walkie-talkie. "I've got her. She'll be on set in fifteen," I heard her say.

Then she turned to me. "This costume fit should be super quick. I checked your measurements against Jam's – you two are virtually identical. I don't think we're going to have any problems."

Nicky was waiting in the dressing room, arranging garments on a rack with my name on a label hanging off it.

"You have two dresses," she said to me. "You'll wear them both at once, layered on top of each other."

The inner layer that she handed me to put on first was very light cotton, pale cream with buttons up the front. The outer layer was grey felted wool. Mum was right, they fitted me perfectly. "That bodice is tight," Mum said, checking the fit at the waist and examining the way the shoulder pads sat. "Can you windmill your arms in it?"

I did as she asked. "It's good. I can move OK," I confirmed. I needed full range of movement for the combat scenes.

The last thing they put on me was my chain mail.

"Hold your arms up," Mum instructed as she took the chain mail off the hanger and came over to me.

I stretched my arms up into the air and she stood on a chair to get above me and lowered the chain mail vest down. I felt the weight of the mail fall on my shoulders like sacks of rocks.

"Ugh."

"Is it too heavy?" Mum looked worried. "Gudrun said we had to make it like proper chain mail to be authentic but it's almost eleven kilos! It's a bit much, when you think you'll have to wear it all day."

"No." I shook my head. "No, Mum, it's amazing, it's perfect. It's just like the real thing."

Mum raised an eyebrow at this. "Like you're the expert," she said dryly. She adjusted the chain mail so that it was sitting perfectly and then Nicky slung a belt at my waist, knotting the leather in a loop at the front, and gave me thick fur boots that came up to my knees. Mum passed me my sword.

As soon as it was in my hand I knew him. His name was Hond. Norsemen always name their weapons, remember, and I had named him Hond, because it means "hand", and that was what it felt like when I held him, as if he were an extension of my own hand.

When I say *I* had named him, I mean *she* had. Brunhilda. But her memories were starting to bleed into my own now and so, when the sword was placed into my hand by my mother, I could remember how Brunhilda had felt when her father had first given Hond to her. She had watched him being forged. Her father had smithed the metal himself, pumping the bellows on the forge to ignite the heat of the burning coals.

So now here I was, with Brunhilda's beloved Hond in my grasp. And even though my transformation this time was nothing more than a wig, clothes and props and not a bit like the real transformation that had come first with the Jonsmessa, I still felt *her* power surge in me. And I knew at that moment that I could do this. I was ready to walk out there in front of the cameras and everyone. Ready to lose myself and become *her*.

There was a knock at the door and Lizzie poked her head in.

"We're waiting on set," she said. "It's go-time."

If I had been myself – ordinary old Hilly Harrison – I think the very idea of walking onto a film set in front of a crew of dozens of people would have freaked me out. But I wasn't me any more when I walked out there. I was Bru. Not just on the surface. It went deeper than that. I held myself taller in that wig and costume. I walked differently. I had her confidence, her swagger. I walked right out there onto the set and stepped out in front of them like Brunhilda would have stepped onto the sacred rock at the All-Thing to claim her crown – as noble and self-assured as a queen, my head high, my gaze unwavering.

Niamh, who was standing with Hammer waiting for me, couldn't believe it.

"Get a look at you! I actually thought you were

Jamisen O'Brien when you first walked out here. You've got some attitude on you!"

She stared quizzically at me. "Have they put contact lenses in? Your eyes have turned very blue."

I didn't answer her, but took the reins and swung myself up onto Hammer's back. "Is Anders on board yet?"

Niamh nodded. "He's at the end of the woods. He wanted to get some practice time with Ollie. I'll take you down there now."

As we walked through the trees, Niamh talked me through the stunt. We'd already done a dry run several times before, but a few things had changed with the pink papers that had been handed out last night.

"Katherine has altered the opening of the scene so now you'll already be in a gallop when you enter the frame. You'll begin the stunt off-camera and, as you come through into the clearing, be aware that the cameras are rolling from that point on. Ride straight when you reach your marker and then, at the second marker, which is the big tree, that's when Anders will ride up to overtake you. Make sense?"

I nodded. "So apart from the start, we hit the same marks that we practised in rehearsal?"

"Yes," Niamh said. "Except you'll finish the sword fight by kissing Sigard."

For a moment my newfound Brunhilda swagger slipped away a little bit but I regained it.

"OK." I took a deep breath. "Sure, no problem."

I could see Anders up ahead of me now on Ollie. He'd been in hair and make-up already that morning too. His blond hair had been groomed back and set into a quiff, braided down the sides, Viking-style. It looked fierce on him and Bobbi had also drawn tattoos all over his arms, which showed beneath his chain mail.

"Hey, Hilly!" He high-fived me as I rode Hammer up alongside Ollie. "You look awesome as a blonde. Ask them if you can keep the wig!"

"Thanks," I said.

"So do you want to hear my plan?"

"Sure," I said nervously.

"OK. So I figure we nail the whole stunt in a single take and make it so perfect they have no choice but to give us the rest of the day off. Then we can go to Blue Lagoon for hot dogs. What do you say?"

"I like that plan," I said. "Can we manage it in one take, though?"

"A couple of pros like us?" Anders grinned. "Course we can."

He moved Ollie into position and I rode past him to take my marker on Hammer, my stomach lurching as I pulled to a halt. In a moment, the cameras were going to start rolling and a multimillion-dollar movie was about to start filming, with me and Anders Mortenson. No pressure!

"Are you OK?" Lizzie asked.

"I think I'm going to be sick," I told her.

"We don't have budget for that," Lizzie replied.

Her coldness shook me out of my nerves and I was steely Brunhilda again.

"Let's do it," I said.

Lizzie took up her position alongside us, clipboard in hand, and spoke into her headset.

"We're good to go here, Katherine. On your command."

I heard the headset crackle. Lizzie looked at me.

"OK, Hilly? Anders? Are we good?"

I turned Hammer around and gave a thumbs-up sign over my shoulder to Anders.

"I'll be right behind you." He smiled.

"I know." I smiled back.

Then I turned to Lizzie and put my game face on. No more smiling. I was in battle mode.

Lizzie spoke into her headset. "Brunhilda forest scene, take one… And… action!"

As she snapped her clapperboard, Hammer leapt forward on cue. His instinct was to break into a tölt but instead I took control and pushed him straight into a gallop. We didn't need his Icelandic paces in this scene – Katherine wanted a good old-fashioned gallop for this part of the movie and Hammer delivered, breaking into stride at full speed, neck arched and knees driving like pistons beneath him.

"Good boy!" I encouraged him to stay with it. The gallop stride didn't come naturally to him – he had been kept to a tölt all his life – so to maintain it now I had to keep my legs on him, asking for more speed to keep him powering forward. We had already passed the first marker and now the cameras were rolling on us. This was it! From here on in, any mistake I made would take us back to square one.

I sat steady in the saddle and, at the second marker, I did as Niamh had told me and took both the reins to my left hand so I could free up my right hand to unsheathe my sword. When I heard the thunder of hooves moving up behind me, I instinctively wanted to turn back and see how close Anders was now. Had he hit his cues behind me on Ollie as we'd planned? But if I turned, that would ruin everything. I couldn't look back at him, and I couldn't catch a glimpse to the left either where right now a tracking camera on a quad bike was keeping pace with Hammer to keep us in shot. All I could do was look straight ahead and prepare for my next marker. I kept my eyeline through the trees and held Hammer steady as I focused on reaching the clearing up ahead between the groves of spruce.

We entered the clearing, timing it perfectly – Anders was suddenly there moving up beside me on Ollie. He came up alongside us, and I held Hammer back so that the horses were now matching each other stride for stride. Anders made the move look easy, to get the horses to sync in together so perfectly, but I could see how hard he was working to get Ollie into stride and stay close to me. We were pressed right up against each other so our knees were touching. I cast a sideways glance to check that he was ready for the next move and Anders gave me a wink! Later, he would insist that he knew the camera would never pick up his facial expression at that moment so it was no big deal, but I didn't know that. If the camera had picked up my expression in response, they would have seen me gawping at Anders in open-mouthed shock.

Our knees were still touching and it was as if our horses were one eight-legged beast as we wound in and out between the boughs of the tree.

Anders stretched out his arm and it looked for a moment as if he were about to take my hand in a grand romantic gesture. And then, with a flourish, he drew his sword.

I drew mine too. There was a moment of impact as our blades connected and the clash of metal was so forceful it threw me back in the saddle. I had to grab at Hammer's neck for a moment to regain my balance. Anders made it look as if the mistake had been intentional. As I fell onto Hammer's neck, Anders slashed his sword above my head, sweeping the air just above me. I sat upright again and swung back at him, all the while keeping Hammer galloping. Anders swung again, sword swooping through thin air, as I raised my right arm back high above my head and swung at him again. It was a close thing when the sword's trajectory came within inches of his throat and it would have connected too if Anders hadn't hit his cue absolutely spot on at that moment and pulled Ollie back, to shorten the black stallion's stride, so that my blade cleaved through the air directly in front of him without drawing blood.

I rode on hard now – my next blow required me to get a little bit ahead of Ollie's strides to deliver an uphand sweep. As I twirled the sword, there was a new confidence in the way I wielded the blade. I'd only trained with Hond and Niamh a handful of times, and yet I was able to brandish my sword like I was a reincarnated Viking warrior. Which I guess I almost was. This was Brunhilda's training, not my own, that was coming out in me. Her Viking blood spurred me to go on the offensive and to finish the fight, so that when Anders parried me back, I had to control myself to resist lunging at him for real. Just in time, I stopped myself from striking him again and again, as if he truly were my sworn enemy. My blood was up, just as Brunhilda's had been that day when she had stuck her blade in the groove of Steen's jugular. If the camera had caught my face at that moment, it would have captured the passion that possessed me. I had to control myself – remember that this was a movie.

As we pulled the horses up, I think that Anders sensed

that our exchange had become almost serious. I was raining blows on him and he had to use his full strength to block my blade as I came at him again and again. When I took a swing at the exact same time he did, and our weapons clashed and locked together, we were entwined in a deadly embrace, pressed up against each other, face to face. I felt my sword bend back. He was too strong for me. But then Hammer gave a snort and reared up and at the same time I managed to wrench my wrist upwards and pull free from Anders, taking his sword up and away with me so that it jerked clean from his hand and fell to the ground.

Disarmed, Anders pulled Ollie around, swinging the stallion on his hocks and making him go up into a rear to face Hammer. Then he raised his right arm over his head and dramatically pulled free the axe he'd been carrying all this time on his back before wheeling it in a circle above his head.

I didn't hesitate. I urged Hammer straight at him. Before Anders had a chance to swing the axe at either of us, I threw myself from my horse's back and landed on top of Ollie in front of the saddle, wrapping both my arms around Anders' waist.

The force of my body against him made Anders

drop the axe and he fell to the ground. Still clinging onto him, I fell too, and the next thing I knew I was lying on top of him in the snow.

I lay there for a moment, a little winded by the fall, catching my breath. We were both weaponless now, face to face in each other's arms. I could feel Anders' breath on my skin, warm and sweet. I adjusted myself in his arms but I made no attempt to get up and I didn't try to fight. I held his gaze, taking in the blueness of his eyes and then he smiled at me and the whole world fell away and I wasn't afraid any more. My heart was racing in all the right ways and I was ready to do this.

"And… cut!" Lizzie's voice came over the loudhailer.

There was a heavy round of applause from the crew.

"Perfect!" Katherine said. "Really great, Hilly! Anders, you stay where you are. Can we get Hilly out of there now and bring Jam in?"

"You're done for the day, Hilly," Lizzie said to me, offering me her hand to help me clamber up to my feet. "A perfect take. Jam is here now to shoot the end of the scene."

And so I stood there and watched, as Jamisen O'Brien, Hollywood's most adorable superstar, positioned herself in the snow, lying with her breastplate against the chest of Anders Mortenson in exactly the spot I had been just moments before. When Lizzie called "Action!" she got her close-up moment and kissed him.

It took Jamisen eleven takes to get that kiss between them just right. Eleven takes for a kiss! Really? It had only taken me one take to ride an entire fight scene.

While they were kissing for the cameras, I was left to take Hammer and Ollie back to their stalls. There, I rubbed them down and rugged them up, giving them their feed before I put my own clothes back on and went back to the hotel.

If ever I had wanted to escape from this world it was right now, and so I headed for the library. I didn't need Gudrun for this. I was certain I could do the ritual alone. And where was the harm? I'd told Gudrun I would wait until I was strong enough again – and today I'd proved I was. I was ready to go back again.

I sat down in the chesterfield chair beside the polar bear and let my fingers run over the indentations made by the buttons in the leather upholstery. The fire was alight, but the embers were low, almost extinguished. I threw on two more logs from the wood pile and, using the poker, stoked the flames until they sparked to life and rose up the chimney. There was a flicker, a rainbow arc of colour above the flames, and my eyes were mesmerised by it. I looked deeper, willing myself inside the flames as they moved, allowing myself to sink deep until my body was consumed by the light and I was nothing but fire myself. And then I was rising up, like the woodsmoke into the air. Suddenly, in a rush of water, the flames were extinguished.

I looked up and saw Hannecke standing over me. She'd doused the fire and had a determined look on her face.

"Bru," she said, "it's time for us to go."

CHAPTER 9

Prince Sigard

Steen and Frey will try and single us out, make us vulnerable before they attack. And so we move as a pack, all of us watching each other's back. The newcomers, Alf and Kari, were Steen's men until now. I let them keep and carry their own swords as a show of my trust, to prove that they are with us now and I'm not afraid that they may betray me.

We take it in turns to bear the weight of Finn on our shoulders. His blood loss has weakened him and his cheeks are so pale. At one point when Kari is holding him, Finn stumbles and falls to his knees.

"Leave me here and go on without me," Finn says, refusing Kari's hand to help him up again. "I'm slowing you all down. My wound is fatal, I think."

We all laugh at his melodrama. "Pull yourself together, Finn! Your wound is an arrow piercing and you'll heal," I say. "Don't think you're going to be admitted to Odin's table at Valhalla with such a minor scrape. And don't ever think that we would leave one of our own here to die. It's not much further. Now get up!"

I reach down and pull him up off the ground and the rest of the way I'm the one that bears his weight on my shoulders.

We're almost there. We've come back to the end of the island where we moored the longboats this morning. Here, the island is exposed to strong winds from the south so that the scattering of skinny trees that have dared to grow among the salty tussock grass are permanently bent over in submission. We're clear of the woods and the plateau is nothing but tussock grass all the way to the cliff edge where the rock face drops away to the sea. There's nowhere to hide here so Steen can't possibly get close without being seen.

"Form a circle," I tell my warriors and we sit down with our backs to each other so that we look out in all directions, keeping a watch for the approach of my brother and Frey.

The tussock grass sways in the wind, rippling like ocean

waves. My eyes scan to the east and then the west, and back again.

"Look! There!"

It is Hannecke who sees them first. She's always had the best eyes of any of us.

"To the east," she whispers to me. "Do you see the way the tussock grass moves? It's them – I'm sure of it!"

I see it too – the unnatural wave in the surface of the long grass. Steen is crawling low on his belly through the tussock grass and Frey is behind him. They aren't visible but you can see the pattern they make, their bodies like centipedes squirming as they make their way to us.

I stand up, and drop my weapons.

"Steen!" I call out. "Is this how you want to do battle? Creeping through the grass like a coward to attack? You can choose another path. Stand up now. Face me in honour! Let's settle this here and now, just you and me, in the Hazelled Field."

My words hang in the air and all that can be heard is the wind whipping at the tussock grass and the sea on the cliffs below, crashing and falling as the waves smash at the rocks. I hold my breath and wait. Beside me, crouching down low, still holding her crossbow, Hannecke has her eyes locked on the point where we last saw Steen in the grass. She's itching to take aim and loose an arrow, but I give her a glance that says, "Wait. Just a little longer..."

And then, out of the grass, no more than a few horse lengths in front of us, Steen stands erect. He has his sword and an axe and he holds both weapons out in front of him. As he locks eyes with me, he drops them to the ground.

Steen glares at me. "The last time we fought one to one you got lucky, Bru," he growls. "This time, I'm not holding back. You want to fight me on the Hazelled Field? Then prepare to lose."

"I don't know why you're doing this," Hannecke says. "We've already taken two of his men and we outnumber him. I could have shot your brother just now in the grass with my arrow – him and Frey too, and this would all be over."

"He is an idiot, my brother," I say. "But he's my brother all the same."

Better that Steen stays alive. And Frey too. I don't want to kill if I don't have to. And who knows? If we did fight, perhaps they might get lucky and take one of us down, too. If this duel goes according to plan, no one needs to die.

The Hazelled Field is marked out by sticks of hazel bough. The space is three metres square. For two warriors fighting in this marked territory the borders are so tight there's hardly enough room to swing a sword. Even less room to avoid being struck by one. But the rules of the Hazelled Field forbid you from stepping outside of the branch boundaries. One foot outside and you've lost the contest.

I take Hond and rotate him in my fist, feeling the weight of my sword, checking the balance of the blade in my grip. I can fight with either hand but I prefer my right, so I use my left to pick up the shield.

In the Hazelled Field we are allowed one weapon each, and one shield to protect ourselves. The contest begins when we both step inside the square and it ends when one of us is forced out of it.

I walk over the hazel bough and stand in the centre. "Go, Bru!"

I glance over and see Hannecke sitting with the others.

She looks anxious. I give her a nod and raise my sword to her as if to say, "I'm going to be OK."

Steen walks warily around the perimeter, looking at me as if I'm a beast in a cage. He's trying to psych me out. It won't work. I know my brother. He thinks he's a cunning warrior but I can read him so easily. In a moment he'll pretend to step forward and then he will...

Lunge! Steen comes at me with the point of his sword and I parry it away and step inside him, twisting myself so that I can make a stab of my own. It strikes his chain mail just above the ribcage but it doesn't pierce through and now Steen turns back on me so that we're facing each other square, chest to chest.

I don't hesitate. With a battle cry, I throw myself at him, hack-hack-hacking away to try and strike his left shoulder, but he has his shield well positioned and I cannot break through. Now he shoulder-barges me. He tries to use his weight to push me so that the momentum will take me backwards to the hazel bough behind me and my foot will step outside the field and end the contest.

It's a weak move. I sidestep to get him off me and backtrack so that once again I'm standing in the centre of the field of combat. Steen gives a ferocious growl and comes at me. He hacks with his sword – great swooping side blows – trying to work around my shield to wound me. He fights so much like a pale imitation of our father! What he lacks, though, is Father's cool head. I can see how he grows frustrated as he keeps hacking and getting nowhere and I position myself right at the very edge of the Hazelled Field. Steen unleashes a battle cry that becomes a full-throated scream and he charges at me like a bull. He's going to use his shield to push me out. As he comes lumbering I wait until the very last moment before dropping to the ground. Bracing myself on my elbows, I swoop out my leg right in front of him. Steen, who has committed to his crazy battle plunge, doesn't have time to change trajectory. He trips over my leg and stumbles forward to the edge of the field. As he falls, I see his eyes meet mine and for the first time I witness undisguised hatred in them, pure loathing for me, as he plummets to the ground and his body collapses across the wrong side of the line.

There's whooping and hollering from my team and I'm panting with exhaustion and grinning from ear to ear at the victory when, suddenly, I hear a sickening whoosh right beside my ear and I see the arrow that has been loosed strike its target.

Hannecke has shot Steen. Her arrow has pierced through the fleshy bulb of his forearm!

At first, I'm filled with horror at her unlawful attack. And then, I see the dagger that is lying beside Steen, the one that a moment ago he'd pulled out from his boot, ready to plunge into me. My brother had a second weapon! And he was planning to stab me – except Hannecke had been too quick for him.

Steen is gripping his arm and whimpering as the blood pours out.

I bend down and pick up his dagger and shove it into my own bootstrap.

"You lose," I tell him, spitting on the ground in front of him. "Now kneel before your sister and your queen."

Steen looks around at all of us. He's still hugging his injured arm, and his red cheeks are streaked with a coward's tears. He looks at Kari, Alf and Frey, as if he expects one of them to step between us to defend him, but no one does. Instead, one by one, these boys who fought beside him cross their right arm over their chest and they drop to one knee.

"Brunhilda!" they say. "Queen of Iceland!"

"Brunhilda!" Hannecke, Erik and Finn lower themselves before me, too.

Only Steen and myself remain standing. And I turn to my brother and see the hatred in his eyes as he accepts his fate and crosses his arm to his chest in allegiance and drops a knee.

"Brunhilda, my sister…" and then, with great bitterness, he says, "my sister, my queen."

I've beaten Steen, so when my father's rule is over I'll take the throne and I will be queen.

We ride the longboats back, exhausted and licking our wounds but happy too, and that night, as the feast at the All-Thing is prepared for us to celebrate, with wild boar being roasted and vegetables cooked in the boiling water of the natural hot springs, Hannecke and I leave the others to go and check on the horses. As we walk across the fields, out of earshot of the others, she shares her concerns about Steen.

"He would have killed you if I hadn't put an arrow in his arm," she says. "He can't be trusted."

"He's my brother," I reply. "I can't kill him. What can I do?"

"Banish him," Hannecke says without pity. "You won't be safe as long as he lives within the tribe."

"Hannecke –" I take her hand – "you are loyal and fearless. But you worry too much. Steen's having trouble getting over the fact that he lost, but he'll accept it with time."

Jotun isn't grazing when we arrive. He stands motionless, his wise head held aloft and ears pricked. When he catches sight of me, he tölts forwards before I even have the chance to call him. He buries his muzzle into my arms and I hold him tight.

"I told you I would come back," I murmur. "And I have news, Jotun. I'm to be queen after my father. What do you think of that? You are to be the queen's stallion."

Hannecke is worried about her horse, Mari. The mare seems to be lame in the near fore and so we trot her up and check the leg for heat.

"I think it might be in the foot," I say. "I can't feel anything in the tendons. She stood on a stone, perhaps?"

"Hopefully she will be sound by tomorrow when we leave..." Hannecke's voice trails off. "Who is that?"

There's a figure running across the fields towards us.

"It's Liesl," I say. I give her a wave. Liesl waves back and keeps running to us.

"Bru!" She's out of breath, heaving to get the words out.

"He's here. He has arrived!"

"What are you on about?" I ask her, confused.

"Prince Sigard," Liesl says. "Your betrothed, the Prince of Greenland, is here at Thing-Vellir!"

So he's come. And who asked him? I wonder. Is it a coincidence that Sigard should turn up now? Just as I've won the right to be queen after my father.

I reach Thing-Vellir with Hannecke at my side, her hand resting on her sword, and Liesl, unarmed and giggling like a twit at the sight of the prince's landing party. He has brought twenty men with him on the longboat from Greenland. They are strong, strapping Vikings. Sigard, on the other hand, is still a boy. He's not much older, if any older, than me. He's taller than Steen and almost as tall as my father. I notice this because the three of them stand together deep in conversation when I arrive.

"Brunhilda!" my father calls out to me. "Come! My daughter, I want you to meet Prince Sigard!"

I walk over to join them. Sigard smiles and nods gallantly but his eyes lock on me with a look as if I'm a cow he's just purchased from a farmer and I stiffen and glower at him.

"Brunhilda," he says. "Congratulations! Your father says you won the Holmgang."

I look at the sour expression on Steen's face and I direct my words at him. "I got lucky..." I say, "...yet again."

Prince Sigard laughs at this. "So much luck! I'm impressed that Odin favours you so greatly. Would it be pushing my luck to ask you to sit with me at the feast tonight?"

My father looks pleased. "Brunhilda is an excellent cook, by the way," he says.

"No, I'm not," I say.

Sigard smiles. "I am sure you are good at anything you want to do, Brunhilda," he says. He's very charming, I suppose, and nice-looking, if you like that sort of thing.

The food is glorious that night at the feast and I'm starving after the Holmgang. I sit with Hannecke to my left and Prince Sigard to my right. Liesl is at the table at the other end of the hall and she spends the whole night staring at Sigard. I thought she was supposed to be in love with my dumb brother!

I eat several helpings of the wild boar and wipe the meat juices off my face with my hands as I chew on the bones.

"You've got an appetite," Sigard says. "I shall have to remember to make sure we have plenty of boar at our wedding feast. And puffin. Do you like puffin?"

"Wedding feast?" I put down my half-gnawed bone.

"We're to be married," Sigard says. "It's all arranged."

I look at him, my face blank in disbelief. "You haven't asked me to marry you. And I haven't said yes."

Sigard laughs. "It's not your job to say yes. Your father is the one who grants permission and he has freely given you to me."

"My father," I say, "is the king. But when he hands on the throne, I will be queen. So I think I have a say in my own destiny."

Sigard looks puzzled.

"He hasn't told you?" he says.

"Told me what?"

Sigard puts his fingertips together to make a steeple, as if he's very serious in his thoughts, which comes across as kind of pretentious. "I think you need to speak to the king. It's not my place to interfere."

I cannot stand up and leave my place during the feast,

but as soon as the meal is over I shoot up from the table to seek out my father. He's resting on goatskins by the fireside with his men.

"Brunhilda!" he says. "Good, good, I was thinking we needed to talk. Come and sit with me!"

He gives the signal to his men that they should leave. I sit down beside him and he puts his big bear-like arm around me. "I saw you at dinner tonight with Sigard. He's a fine-looking boy, isn't he? And he'll make a good king. I'm glad you two are getting on so well."

I look at my father with hurt and betrayal in my eyes. "Sigard told me I'm going to marry him. He said it was your doing."

"Ah," my father said. "Yes, well... here's the thing, Brunhilda. If you wed Sigard, the marriage will strengthen our two lands with its union. And it solves my little problem here in Iceland. Your brother has been complaining ever since the Holmgang. Now, if you marry Sigard, Steen can take the throne here when I die and you can move to Greenland as Sigard's queen. My two children will be on the thrones of both countries – Steen as ruler after me and you as Sigard's bride."

"Are you serious?" I can't believe what I'm hearing. "But I won the Holmgang! Iceland should be mine."

"And what would your brother do in this design of yours?" my father says. "He would have no crown."

"He doesn't deserve a crown," I reply. "He can't lead and he can't follow either. He's a twit. He's not fit to be a king."

My father turns quiet. "He's the male heir," he says. "Be thankful you will still be a queen. It's a very important position, to be the wife of a ruler."

"But I'm *the* ruler not the wife!" I say. "It should be me, not Steen. And I don't want to go to Greenland. I don't want to leave here! I have Jotun and Hannecke. This is my home."

"You'd be wise to watch the way you speak to me." Father's expression is stern. "Your future is decided. One day you will become Sigard's bride. But, for now, you're still my daughter. I'm still king and Iceland is still your home."

I leap to my feet. "This is the sort of trick that the god Loki might play," I say. "You'll be sorry. Steen is not the true heir to your throne, and you will regret your decision to choose him. And as for me, I will never, ever forgive you."

"Brunhilda!" I hear him calling me back but I don't stop. I'm too angry. I storm away from the party and through the valley. The only one I want to see right now is my horse. Jotun is not going to believe this!

"He has betrayed me," I tell him as I arrive at my stallion's side.

Jotun lowers his muzzle and wraps his neck round me to comfort me. I grab his mane in my fingers; the bright golden-red strands are almost luminous in the night air, the sky deep pink and mauve above us. It will get dark tonight, I think, perhaps for several hours. Summer's endless days are gone. The winter is coming.

I sit with Jotun for a long time and I think about my fight with my father. He's been king for a long time. It was his strength that made him king, but it's wisdom that keeps him on the throne. He's moving me like a chess piece, protecting his people by marrying me off to Sigard. That way Steen can have Iceland and our family's bloodline will one day rule Greenland too. The truth is, my father knows deep down that my brother is an idiot, but he's still the male heir. The crown was always going to go Steen's way. I should never have defied Father like that. Better to stay close to him and have his ear, and try to talk him round. Perhaps I can change his mind before he sends me away to Greenland.

"But if all else fails and I must go," I say to Jotun, "I'm taking you with me in the longboat and you will become a Greenland stallion."

Jotun doesn't look pleased about this at all. He gives a miserable snort.

"Yes," I say, "me too. But if we have to live in Greenland, at least we'll have each other."

I stroke his muzzle. "Let's not think about it any more," I console him. "It may be years away yet before Steen takes over as king."

In the morning I'll go to Father and apologise, tell him that I'm sorry for my outburst. It's too late to see him now. He will have retired to his tent. It must be past midnight.

I'll sleep here tonight, on the grass next to Jotun. I throw down the goatskin I had wrapped around my body and I'm about to lie down when Jotun begins to act strangely. His nostrils widen and then he raises his head to the sky and lets out a stallion's clarion call.

"Jotun? What is it? What is wrong?"

And then I hear voices. There's shouting and wailing coming from the sacred rock.

I grab hold of Jotun's mane at the wither and I use it

to cling to as I spring up and mount him bareback, swinging my leg high over his rump. Once I'm on board I kick him on, into a tölt.

In the darkness, I'm relying on his sure-footedness as we move swiftly through the valley, towards the campsite. I can see the men of our tribe gathered at the entrance to my father's tent, the lights of fire torches in their hands.

"What is going on?" I ask, flinging myself down from Jotun's back and running towards them. I see that they are guarding the entrance and I try to push past them to force my way inside.

"Hold her!" one of the men says. "No one may enter!"

"What do you mean?" I shout. "I'm the daughter of the king!"

"You were the daughter of the king."

It is my brother who speaks to me.

Steen and Sigard stand together with the men of our tribe behind them.

"Kneel, Bru, and bow to me," Steen says darkly. "Our father is dead. I'm your king now."

I should have seen it coming. I should have known that Steen and Sigard were in conspiracy. They're both murderers, that's what they are. But this doesn't seem to matter to anyone but me. The old and the weak die, the young and the strong take their place. It's cold-blooded but it's the Viking way.

"Make a funeral pyre," Steen says, as if he's a good and loyal son. "Let us send the king to Valhalla."

They build my father a raft made out of logs, and pile a stack of branches on top. Then they bring his body out of the tent and place it upon it. And while the night sky is still dark, they carry the raft down the length of Thing-Vellir until we have once again reached the sea-lake. Here they wade out into the water until they are waist-deep and then they set it afloat.

I run into the water and climb on board the raft. Clutching his cold hand, I kiss the golden band on his finger. "I'm sorry, Father," I say, "I will always regret that the last words we spoke were in anger." And then I growl, "But I was right. Steen isn't fit to rule after you. If you had listened to me and not trusted him, you would still be alive."

I clamber back down from the raft and stand waist-deep in the freezing water as the men set it alight with torches, pushing the raft out into the sea. And as I watch the flames burn, I feel myself captured by their flicker. The flames have me drawn deep within them. I'm transcending, leaving this place. And this time, as my heart breaks with grief, I am glad to be gone.

CHAPTER 10

The Fire Ring

Death is a glorious thing to a Viking. I remember, not long after Anders and I had first met, that day when we'd walked together and we'd eaten lingonberries. We had talked about dying then and I'd told him what Gudrun had said to me, about how important it was to the Vikings to be noble when you left the world.

"It's the moment of judgment," I'd said to him, "when Odin the All-Father sends his Valkyries to fetch you – they were these angel-women who flew down from heaven to collect the fallen from the battlefield. If you died like a hero, the Valkyries would lift you up to Valhalla, where Odin and Thor and the other gods all lived, and you would feast at the table with the gods and be immortal forever."

"What about horses?" Anders said. "Do you think horses go to Valhalla?"

"I guess so. Why?"

"Because I wouldn't want to go there without my horse," Anders said. "I wouldn't want to spend eternity without Ollie, you know?"

His words made me feel like someone was squeezing my chest. All of a sudden I couldn't breathe properly.

Anders looked at me. "Hey, what's up?"

"Nothing."

"Did I say something wrong?" Anders said. "I didn't mean to upset you."

"No, it's not your fault," I replied.

"So what is it?" Anders said.

I took a deep breath and wiped my face to get rid of the hot, warm tears.

"You remember when you got here, how I told you that I had a pony at home?"

"Piper?" Anders said. "Yeah, of course I remember you told me about her. She got colic, right? That's why you couldn't event this season?"

I nodded. "I've been trying not to think about her since I got here."

Anders put his arm round me. "It's OK," he said,

"I know you miss her, but it's not forever. Once we finish filming we'll be going home and you'll be with her again."

I looked at him. "No," I said truthfully. "I won't."

There's a reason why I don't like to talk about what happened that night with Piper. I remember the moment that we were on our way to the surgery and it was raining like crazy and the windscreen wipers on the car were going at double speed. I remember how they couldn't keep the rain at bay which was coming like a sheet of water in front of us, but most of all I remember how I was just sobbing my guts out – that was the point at which Mum had said to me that when this was all over she would take me to Iceland. She'd thought at the time that I'd need to go away with her because Piper would take months to recover from the surgery and I wouldn't be able to compete, and going to Iceland would take my mind off things while she recuperated.

But that wasn't what happened.

The surgery for colic is huge and complicated. They

sedate the horse and then, once they're knocked out, they winch them up on to the operating table.

I tried not to think too hard about how scary the surgery was while Piper was on the table. Mum and I had sat in the waiting room and we truly didn't speak one word to each other for hours. I'd tried to watch the TV hanging on the wall but it was middle-of-the-night infomercials. When the vet came out at last and said that they'd done their best to remove the blockage, and Piper was now coming out of the anaesthetic and they would keep her overnight in their stalls, and we should go home and get some sleep and come pick her up tomorrow, I was so relieved I started sobbing all over again, but with tears of joy this time.

So we took her home. The vet gave us instructions. A small turnout paddock, no hard feed, lots of water with molasses in it to make her drink and two biscuits of hay a day to get her slowly eating again.

"The thing is," I told Anders, "if the colic is really bad, then sometimes after the surgery, even if you take super-good care of them, it can come back again. And if it does come back, then there's nothing they can do…"

"And that's what happened to Piper?" Anders asked.

"Not straight away. I mean, for almost a week she was fine. She'd pulled through the surgery and she was moving around and eating and everything. I thought she was totally OK. Then one day after school I went out into the paddock. She was down on the ground again and I just knew. I just knew that this time it was bad."

Mum and I stayed with her until the vet came, I explained. I was cradling her head in my lap and she was making these pitiful snorts and there was a froth of sweat on her neck. She was trembling because she was in so much pain. Then when the vet got there and saw her and took her pulse and her temperature, she turned to Mum and said, "Can I speak with you over here for a moment?"

And Mum got up and they both walked away from me to talk, even though she's my pony and I should have been allowed to discuss things too. And when they came back, Mum said, "Hilly, you need to go in the house now…"

"Your mum had to make a tough decision," Anders said. "She was only trying to protect you…"

"I know…"

I had to stop and take a deep breath because I was about to start sobbing all over again. And I wanted to finish and tell Anders all of it.

"When she told me to go, I just turned my back and went inside and I left Piper with them, and as I was walking away I knew. I knew what they were doing. I knew she was going to die. But I couldn't say goodbye and I couldn't stay. How could I watch them do that to her…"

I was crying so hard now I couldn't speak, I could barely breathe.

"It's OK, Hilly." Anders held me tight.

"No, it's not," I sobbed. "I shouldn't have left. I should have stayed there and been with her until the end. I mean, she was my pony. You don't just walk away like that if you truly love someone…"

The tears were choking my throat now. I wiped my face furiously with my hand. I was useless! I'd been no good to Piper then and, now, here I was crying about it like some self-indulgent kid!

"Hey, hey, come here." Anders took my tear-stained hands and held them in his own. "Stop beating yourself up for this, Hilly. Piper was lucky to have someone like you. And if there's one thing she did know right at the end, it's how much you loved her. I'm sure of it."

Those were the conversations I had with Anders Mortenson. So if I didn't get the chance to kiss him, I didn't really care. As far as I was concerned, what we had between us was better than a Hollywood movie.

The weird thing about working on a film is that they don't create the whole thing in sequence, like you see on the screen when it's finished. The filming schedule is all out of order, so it's hard to get an idea of how much of the movie you've got done and how much there's still to come. All I knew was that Mum had originally said we'd be in Iceland for almost two months and now there was less than two weeks to go. There were still some major scenes to be shot though – including the fire ring.

I remembered Gudrun describing the ring, the night we first met. "It's a symbol of her enchantment. Brunhilda is thrown into a deep sleep and she's trapped inside a burning ring of fire so that no one can reach her," Gudrun said. "Then Prince Sigard comes for her on his horse and awakens her with a kiss."

"Like *Sleeping Beauty*?"

"There are similarities," Gudrun admitted. "They say the original story of the fairy tale is based on *her*, but it has been contorted, so we do not know the truth."

That conversation seemed so long ago now. Bru and I, we'd been through so much since then. I knew her nature now and, if there was one thing I was certain of, it was that she wasn't the sort of girl who lies there and waits for a kiss to rescue her.

"Prince Sigard murdered her father," I said. "He's not some hero come to rescue her. She doesn't want anything to do with him!"

Gudrun and I were sitting in the library together. She'd arrived before me and had the fireplace prepared, but even though it was cold tonight and wet outside, we didn't dare to light it in case I mistakenly transported back once more. I'd confessed to Gudrun that I'd gone back again without her. She had been concerned about this, but she was even more concerned about what I'd discovered.

"This is very serious," she said when I told her the truth about Steen and Sigard's treachery again King

Erik. "Hilly, what you've found out, what you are telling me – it's the opposite of everything the scholars believed about Brunhilda."

"I know," I said. "And now we're about to film this big Hollywood ending, where Sigard leaps through a wall of flames on Ollie's back to rescue Bru, and it's just not true. It didn't happen like that. Bru despises him!"

Gudrun frowned. "We have to go and talk to Katherine… before it's too late."

A film crew is like a kingdom all of its own and, in our little world here at the Isbjörn hotel, Katherine Kara was the queen. Even Gudrun, who had Katherine's ear more than anyone else in the crew, didn't have the power to just walk up and knock on her door. We had to go to Lizzie to set us up a meeting.

"Katherine's looking at rushes tonight," Lizzie told us. "She said she couldn't be disturbed."

"She'll want to see us," Gudrun insisted. "We have very important matters to discuss."

"Sorry." Lizzie shook her head. "She's in lockdown

mode right now. We're so far behind on the shooting schedule the studio is demanding to see footage and she needs to deliver. I'll see what I can do but she doesn't want to be interrupted by anyone."

I got the feeling Lizzie was enjoying saying this to Gudrun. I knew she was in the same camp as my mum and Jimmy, the assistant director – they all thought Gudrun's witchy ways had too much influence on Katherine and that Gudrun did nothing but slow down the filming.

"Well, it's on Lizzie's head," Gudrun grumbled to me. "We're supposed to be filming the fire ring scene tomorrow. I know that once I tell her what we've discovered Katherine is going to want to shut down production while we figure out what to do instead."

I went to bed that night without mentioning anything to Mum. I knew she'd been working like crazy to get the costumes for the fire ring scene done on time, and I didn't want to say that the scene might not even happen now – not if Gudrun got her way and told Katherine the truth. Katherine trusted Gudrun. Luckily Mum mistook my quietness for nerves.

"You'll be great tomorrow, sweetie," she reassured me.

"Thanks," I said weakly. I was stunt-doubling for Jam

in the fire ring scene. If it went ahead, all I had to do was lie on the marble slab and pretend to be asleep, and then, once Anders woke me, he would take me in his arms and lift me onto Ollie's back and vault on board in front of me. Then I had to wrap my arms around him and he'd jump Ollie out through a hole in the wall of flames, with me as a pillion passenger.

I didn't sleep much. When I met Gudrun at the breakfast buffet I was bleary-eyed.

"No time to eat," she said, taking the plate out of my hand and walking me away from the table. "Lizzie's finally got us in to see Katherine. She's scheduled a ten-minute meeting at 8 a.m. We need to get over to the edit suite now."

When we arrived at the edit suite, Lizzie was there guarding the door. "You've got five minutes max," she said as she let us in. "Katherine's on a tight deadline."

Katherine was in the suite in a swivel chair behind the edit desk, facing the big screen. The room was darkened so that she could focus and flanking her, one on each side, were Jimmy and the editor, whose name was Simon. They all looked like they'd been working all night. There were half-eaten toasted sandwiches and coffee cups strewn over the desk.

"OK, Lizzie said you needed to see me?" Katherine was brisk. "What's up?"

"I've cast the runes…" Gudrun began. But Katherine wasn't in the mood for the long version.

"And… like I said, what's up?"

Gudrun looked at me, as if to say, "Here we go!"

"I've uncovered some new research. It would be historically inaccurate to have Prince Sigard and Brunhilda get married. We need to change the end of the script and cancel the fire scene today."

Jimmy and Simon weren't pretending to ignore us any more. They both swivelled in their chairs too to hear what their director had to say about this.

"You have got to be kidding me!" Katherine shrieked in disbelief. "You come in here at the eleventh hour and want me to get rid of the ending of my movie?"

"I tried to come and see you yesterday," Gudrun said.

Katherine gave a hollow laugh. "You realise there's no way I can do this! I've got a crew turning up on set right now, we're out of time and over budget."

"But you brought me on board to protect the integrity of this project," Gudrun said. "So that's what I'm doing. I believe that Prince Sigard was in part responsible for the death of the king – Brunhilda's father. If we have him marry Brunhilda, despite his treachery, then we're not being true to her."

"So you're telling me you want me to ditch not just this scene but the whole romantic lead," Katherine fumed, "and then alter the ending to... to what exactly?"

"I'm sorry about the timing. Like I said, we tried to see you yesterday," Gudrun said. "And we're not sure what to replace it with. Hilly and I are... still researching."

Katherine glared at me. As if this were all my fault. Then she gave a heavy sigh.

"Gudrun, you know how much I respect your work. I really do. And I've made so many changes to this film based on what you've told me, haven't I? I've always listened to you, even when the rest of the crew were rolling their eyes."

Gudrun nodded. "Yes, Katherine. And I appreciate your drive to keep the movie authentic. That is why I'm asking you to do this very important thing."

Katherine sighed. "I'm sorry, Gudrun. It's just a bridge too far. If the studio discovers that I've suddenly, for no good reason, got rid of the big final scene when they've approved it all, they'll shut us down. Or maybe they'll just fire me and stick someone else in the job. I'm already under so much pressure to deliver this movie on time. Any way that you see it, if it's me or someone else they replace me with, this ending will be the one that happens."

"But…" Gudrun tried to speak but Katherine cut her down.

"I want to be supportive, I really do, but I just can't see a way around this. I can't rewrite an entire movie at this stage. Brunhilda is in love with Sigard, that's what this whole movie is about – their love."

"Then this movie is based on a lie." That was me talking. I don't know what I thought I was doing. I guess I just felt responsible. I had to do what I could. For Bruhilda. "Bru might have thought Sigard was OK at first, but when she finds out that he's killed her father and sided with her brother? There's no way she'd marry him."

Katherine looked at me. She wasn't angry. Her face was an implacable sea of calm.

"You're about to learn a life lesson, Hilly," she said. "All of us, at some point in time, end up doing things that we never thought we would do. And this is a man's world. If Steen did replace his father as king and Sigard ruled Greenland, do you really think Brunhilda would have had a chance against both of them? Maybe you don't like this ending, but it's where she ends up. She's marrying Sigard, and that's the end of the matter."

"I thought a director would have more power than this," Gudrun said.

We were walking back towards the costume rooms. I was due in hair and make-up.

"Katherine's behind schedule and over budget," I replied. "I can see what she means – if she tried to put her foot down, they'd replace her. She can't stand up to them at this late stage."

And then the thought hit me like a lightning bolt. "But what if someone they couldn't replace stood their ground and refused to do the scene?"

Gudrun gave my shoulder a squeeze. "Hilly, that is very noble of you, but it's no good. If you refuse to go on, they'll just use another stand-in for the stunt. Niamh or anyone else in the crew could wear the wig."

"No. I don't mean me," I said to her. "I mean Anders."

"Go talk to him," Gudrun agreed. "You may have a point, and it's our last chance."

Anders was having his hair blow-dried when I walked in. He had his head tilted forward so that Bobbi could work on the nape of his neck.

"Hilly!" he said brightly as he raised his head and saw me reflected in his make-up mirror. "I won't be much longer. Bobbi just has to finish my hair."

Then he saw my face.

"Is something up?"

"Yes," I said. "We need to talk."

Anders let out a low whistle. "I've been in a lot of movies now and, whenever somebody says that line, you can guarantee nothing good is going to happen next."

"I need to ask you to do something for me," I said. "Gudrun and I, we've been doing this research into Brunhilda and we believe she never married Sigard. We think he conspired with Steen to murder the king. Which means this whole fire ring thing, it never really

191

happened, and we've told Katherine but we can't convince her to ditch the fire ring scene."

"And you're coming to me because…"

"You're the only one with enough power to talk to Katherine and make her change her mind. Tell her you'll refuse to film the fire ring scene and then she'll have to go back and make alterations to the script."

Bobbi had switched off the blow-dryer now and she was braiding the sides of Anders' hair, so he had to keep very still and look straight ahead into the mirror as he spoke to me.

"Why are you doing this, Hilly?" he said. "Is it for Gudrun? You know, no one on the crew likes her. They think she's on a power trip. And you – you keep falling for her witchy nonsense."

"I don't." I shook my head. "I'm not doing it for her. I'm doing it for Brunhilda."

Anders took a deep breath. "Brunhilda? A girl who lived thousands of years ago? You don't even know her and yet you want me to throw aside the best scene I have in this movie and literally ask Katherine to remove me as the hero, just because of what you think actually happened?"

"I want you to do what's right," I said. "Bru would never have married Sigard."

"But maybe she did," Anders offered. "Maybe she had no choice. You don't know for sure."

Was he right? It was true – I didn't know for sure what had happened to Bru. Steen and Sigard had killed the king. They were in charge now. Was it possible that her marriage to Sigard, just like in the fairy tale, was her only choice left?

"Please, Anders," I said. "If you refuse to do the scene, the crew will all stand by you, I know they will. They respect you."

Anders stared at the mirror. Bobbi took his make-up cape off and he stood up from the chair. I tried to read his expression, but he was too good an actor for that. He looked at me and his eyes said nothing. "Your turn, Hilly." He gestured to the chair. "I'll see you when you're ready on set."

"So will you talk to her?"

"I need to think about this," Anders said. And he walked out of the trailer and left me there with Bobbi sticking pins in my hair.

All the time I was in Bobbi's chair I was hoping someone would come bursting into the trailer and say there was a change of plan and the day's filming had been cancelled. I began to convince myself that, once Anders thought about this, he would come through for me. So when I reached the set and I couldn't see Anders or Katherine anywhere, my heart leapt.

But then he emerged, in full costume, riding Ollie, with Niamh at his side with a lead rein on the stallion.

"What's going on?" I said to him. "Have you talked to Katherine? What did she say?"

Anders looked at me and at that moment I could see the truth in his eyes, and I knew what he was about to tell me.

"I'm not going to do it, Hilly," he said. "You want me to try and persuade the director to get rid of my best scene? That's like asking me to destroy my own career. I'm sorry, but it's too much to ask…"

"Can we have Hilly on set now, please?" It was Lizzie's voice ringing out officiously. "Places, everyone! We're about to begin shooting. Have we got Hilly? We need you up on the marble table – straight away!"

I didn't move. I looked at Anders, my eyes pleading.

"She's coming!" Anders called out to Lizzie.

And he turned Ollie and rode away to take up his position, ready to begin.

A few things I remember about filming that day – how it took forever for them to get the lighting set up just right, and how I had to lie on that marble slab for what seemed like hours, so that by the time we actually were ready for the cameras I was freezing cold. And then they complained that I was ruining the shot because my lips had turned blue and I was shivering when I was supposed to be almost dead anyway.

In the end they got hot water bottles and laid them all the way down the marble underneath me to warm me up. I was lying in the centre like a perfect corpse on my slab, with my eyes shut tight, when they fixed the fire wall, and I felt the heat of the flames in a circle around me.

I was blind to the world as Lizzie called "Action!" and Anders, as Prince Sigard, set off at a gallop. He rode Ollie straight into the wall of flames which magically parted around him as they jumped inside the ring. He dismounted and threw the horse's reins aside before he rushed over to me, raised me up and held me close in his arms. He stroked my long blonde hair as he told me that love was greater than all things, including death, and that all he desired in the world was for me to return to him now.

I've seen the movie. You can't tell it's really me. My face on the screen is obscured when he bends over and kisses me and, besides, I look just like Jam O'Brien with that wig on. But it was me on that slab, and he did kiss me that day. Anders Mortenson bent down, and he took me in his arms and he kissed me.

Once upon a time, that kiss might have been all I'd ever wanted. Now his lips felt like poison against mine. I remember that kiss. I remember hating every traitorous moment of it and wanting nothing more than for it to be over.

I don't recall much more after that because I made the stupid mistake after he kissed me of opening my eyes. And that was when I realised I was looking straight into the fire ring, and suddenly I wasn't in my own body any more. I was going back again, back to Brunhilda. Transported back through the flames for the last time.

CHAPTER 11

Loki's Trick

The day after I watch my father's body burn, I'm forced to stand at the sacred rock and witness his killer, my brother, being crowned king.

Steen looks ridiculous up there. He's draped in one of my father's furs but it's too big for him. I let out a snigger when the crown lowers onto his head and Steen's brow is too small to hold it, so it slips down to his nose and he has to shove it back up again.

"Bru!" Sigard, my so-called husband-to-be is standing beside me and he tells me off sternly. "Your brother is the king now and we don't laugh at kings."

No, we don't laugh at kings like Steen. We fear them. My brother is vain and dumb and self-absorbed. This is not going to end well. Sigard doesn't know him like I do.

"We need to talk."

"What about?" Sigard says.

"Wedding plans," I reply. This is a lie but it's not safe to discuss the things I have in mind here in Thing-Vellir. "Let's go ride the horses," I say. We can talk that way.

Jotun is always strong in my hands, but today he pulls so hard against me I have trouble keeping him back. His tölt is much swifter than Sigard's horse and in the end I have to be firm with Jotun and halt him and wait for Sigard to catch us up. Jotun frets and snorts, stamping at the ground with impatience.

"Behave!" I caution him. "Be good. We need Sigard on our side. This may be our last chance."

Sigard seems impressed by Jotun's nonsense. "I like a horse with spirit," he says. "He has the fire in his blood as well as his mane."

"He's moody because he doesn't like to be held back," I say. "Perhaps we should walk?"

And so we walk, down through the valley carved out between sheer rock faces, until we are on the plains, a patchwork of rust-brown heather, grey lichen and sage moss. I like it best at this time of year – when the snow has yet to fall in earnest and you can see the land. The streams are trickling but soon winter will freeze them solid. I watch a pair of black ravens pecking dolefully at the ground, hoping to conjure up worms with their beaks.

"You're very quiet for someone who wants to talk," Sigard says.

We've let our reins slip all the way to the buckle and the horses are walking freely, Jotun stretching his neck, snorting and blowing, shaking out his enormous mane.

"All right then," I say. "I wanted to tell you that you've made a mistake siding with Steen. My brother is a halfwit and a brute and now that he's king you're in danger."

"I'm in danger?" Sigard raises an eyebrow.

"Yes," I confirm. "You think because you'll be married to me he'll be happy to trade with Greenland, to treat you as an ally, as my father had planned. But he won't. My brother would sacrifice me in an instant – he's got no family loyalty, as you've seen. Greed and arrogance will get the better of him soon enough and he'll come after you. He'll raise an army to attack you and take Greenland from you."

We pull the horses to a halt. The wind is whipping my hair across my face as I turn to him.

"So let me guess," Sigard says. "You've got a new plan?"

"I have," I say. "You take my side, and my followers and yours join forces. We rise up now against Steen, take the throne back and make me Iceland's queen. Then you and I can each run our own country as allies."

I spit on my hand and then I extend it out to him.

Sigard looks at my hand for a moment, and then he spits on his own palm and we shake. The deal is sealed.

"Tell your warriors to get ready," he says. "We meet at the All-Thing rock at midnight to take back your crown."

As I put on my chain mail that evening, I think about what I'm intending to do. I have fought in single combat, and on the island we fought four-against-four, but I have never been in a full battle like this before. Hannecke and I have spent the day in quiet confidence, taking my followers aside one by one and speaking to them, getting them to pledge their allegiance to me. We have done the head count many times over and we are certain that, if we combine with Sigard's men, we will easily outnumber Steen's handful of loyalists.

I hone the blade of my sword on the sharpening rock and hope that I won't need it. I hate the idea of fighting against my own people, but I'll do it if I have to. And I'll command my men in the same way that my father did, leading from the front on my stallion to face the spears and arrows, the first one to swing my sword against our enemies.

I swear Jotun knows that tonight is special. When I am saddling him up he's usually as still as a statue, but tonight he skips and frets and won't stand for me to tighten the girth.

I'm not afraid of going into battle. Odin is on my side. The only jag of fear in my belly is for Jotun. I love him so much, I want to keep him safe. I dress him in chain mail, buckling it to his breastplate and attaching it to his saddle to protect him from stray arrows. The bronzed armour sparkles against his dark coat and he looks so handsome in it. I put my arm around his neck and bury my face in the fire of his mane.

"When this battle is over," I say to my horse, "we'll go away together along the coast. Just you and me. We'll go on an adventure, galloping through the forests to the sea and then back between the mountain ranges, all the way to the high plains where the wild herds run, and you can eat the sweet moss grasses that grow there and we'll sleep rough and make campfires and it will just be the two of us. No one else. Won't that be fun?"

Jotun swivels his ears and snorts in agreement. I swear he understands me. When I mount up on his back, I feel him bristling with energy. He trots on the spot with excitement as Hannecke assembles our people behind me. Tonight we'll ride as one through Thing-Vellir with shields braced together for protection and our swords slung at our hips and axes strapped to our backs. At the sacred rock we'll gather and meet with Sigard and his men and then, with our forces doubled in strength, we'll ride on together into the main camp where Steen is fast asleep and we'll rouse him and his men from their tents and tell them they must surrender or die. It will be a bloodless coup.

"It's a pity," says Hannecke as she rides alongside me through the valley. "Sigard is handsome enough. He would have been a good husband for you."

I feel my cheeks turn hot as I blush at this. It's not that I don't want to be married some day, and yes, Sigard is not too ugly, I suppose. I would even marry him perhaps, if it were my choice one day. But not like this. Not bartered off by my brother like I'm a possession to be traded.

"There he is," she says.

Sigard is on the rock with his men assembled, waiting for us. There's no going back now.

"You're not being disloyal." Hannecke reads my mind. "Steen has brought this on himself."

Steen! I'm thinking about my brother when I see him emerge in front of me. He rides out from behind Sigard's men, and sits there smiling at me as I approach.

"What's he doing here?" Hannecke reaches for her sword.

Suddenly, from the gloom of the valley around us, we see shapes emerge from the shadows and begin to close in on us. Men on horseback, Steen's men, surrounding us from all sides.

It's an ambush. They knew we were coming!

"Sigard is a double-crosser! I'm going to kill him!" It's Hannecke. She has her sword raised and her eyes are red with anger.

"No," I say. "Calm down, this is not the time or place."

I turn round, stand up in my stirrups and call out to our warriors assembled behind me.

"Sheathe your swords. We are at the sacred rock and you know that it would offend the gods for blood to be spilled here."

I know this law and so does Steen, of course. That must have been why Sigard arranged to meet here. It was his plan all along, to betray me yet another time, here in a place where he knows I will not offend Odin or the other gods by fighting back. We are beaten before we even began.

"Brunhilda." Steen opens his arms to me as I approach. "Little sister. Always so pleased with your cleverness. What was it she called me last night, Sigard?"

Sigard smiles. "She said you were a halfwit."

Steen's face is stony. "Not very nice, Bru. You'll pay for that. And not accurate either, because look which one of us has been fooled. It's not me."

I ignore him and glare at Sigard.

"You'll pay for this betrayal," I hiss at him.

"Oh, Bru!" Sigard laughs. "Come on! Don't be so serious. And don't be angry. I want my bride to be happy."

"I'm not your bride," I snarl.

"Oh, I think you are!" Sigard snaps back. "Tonight you'll

surrender to us and tomorrow there'll be a wedding. We're not wasting any more time on this."

He rides his horse forward and reaches out a hand to grab at my bridle, holding Jotun's head roughly.

"And what a wedding gift you bring me tonight. A stallion with a fire mane. The perfect beast for the fighting pits to celebrate our union."

I reach out and pound my fist on his hand, trying to get him to release Jotun's bridle. "No! Let go of him! He's mine."

"You don't understand, little sister," Steen laughs. "You're not in control any more. Tomorrow we're having a wedding, and Jotun's blood will be our entertainment."

Sigard lets go of my bridle and beckons to his men. "Take the bride away so she can prepare herself for our wedding," he says. Sigard's men ride forward to surround me, their swords held ready to strike.

Hannecke reaches again for her sword to defend me.

"No!" I hiss at her. "They'll kill you. They're Greenlanders and they don't respect the rules of blood at the sacred rock."

Hannecke is fuming as she's forced to sheathe the sword, but she knows I'm right. There's nothing we can do. As they flank us on either side, I ride Jotun forward into the valley, back to our camp so I can pack my bags for Greenland and prepare for my wedding day.

"You can't marry him!" Hannecke is pacing furiously up and down as she watches me pack my bags. "This is an outrage. This whole business. You are the rightful queen."

I keep packing, shoving my heavy fur coat and boots into the bag, and food for the journey: a cheese, some dried reindeer meat and a loaf of bread. I'm going to need provisions.

"We can attack them again tonight," Hannecke insists. "I'll go from door to door and assemble our allies and..."

I grab her by the shoulders. "Hannecke, stop," I say. "You are the most loyal friend I could ever have asked for. I love you so much you're like a sister to me. It would break my heart to see you hurt and that's why I'm asking you to accept this. We're not going to beat them. We've lost. And now, now I need to leave."

Hannecke collapses down on my bed. "So this is it then? Truly? After tomorrow I'm never going to see you again?"

I clasp her hand in mine. "You never know," I say.

"That is for the gods to decide. Meanwhile, I need you to be my friend more than ever before, Hannecke. I have one last favour to ask of you."

My wedding is held in the morning. Along the clifftops that border the valley leading to the rock of the All-Thing, they assemble to watch the marriage between an Icelandic princess and the Prince of Greenland. It's a solemn event, the joining of two royal bloodlines and two countries, and the valley is shrouded in mist, as if adding weight to the seriousness of the proceedings.

On the sacred rock my husband-to-be, Sigard of Greenland, stands and waits for his bride. He's dressed in a golden elk fur that matches his hair and he wears his crown tilted back on his head at an angle that makes the most of his face, the aquiline nose and handsome cheekbones.

I've been given a crown too. It's silver and set with onyx, a gift from Sigard to his bride on her wedding day. It belonged to his mother apparently. I think it's tasteless and vulgar, the onyx is too shiny. It sits on top of my veil, which is heavy damask lace and hangs low all the way to the waist like a shroud, covering my hair and my face.

The bridal walk to the sacred rock is slow, but it still feels too fast if you ask me. What's the hurry? A bride should walk slowly, slowly. Let this wedding march take forever. I have no handmaidens and no father to give me away and so this is a lonely walk to the drumbeat being played to urge my footsteps on.

Finally, the long, slow bridal march is done. On the sacred rock, Sigard steps forwards to stand at my side, ready at last to claim his wife. Steen steps up too and stands in front facing the crowds. He has taken my father's place as celebrant today and he will do the honour of marrying me off.

"You may take her hand," Steen instructs Sigard.

Sigard grunts and reaches out a clammy pale hand to grip my own. Steen takes the rope from his waist and uses it to bind our hands together.

"This rope symbolises your union," he says. "You are husband and wife now."

Steen looks smug. "Lift the veil now, Prince Sigard, and you may kiss your bride."

Sigard leans in for the kiss and with his remaining free hand he reaches out and lifts up the veil.

There's a gasp from the crowd as Sigard recoils and jerks back at the rope that binds his wrist.

Hannecke laughs in delight at his anger. "Oh, my husband!" she says. "It's too late to get cold feet now."

On the rock in front of the bride and groom, Steen is gawping at Hannecke in confusion.

"What is going on here?" He turns round and shouts at the crowd, "Who did this? Where is Bru?"

My brother. He's still not getting it. He really is a halfwit.

Last night, as I sat on the bed with Hannecke and held her hand, I told her my plan.

"Here is how it's going to happen tomorrow. They'll lead me up the valley to the sacred rock of the All-Thing and the ceremony will take place. Then, after I marry Sigard, they're going to celebrate at the wedding feast with a stallion fight. They'll put Jotun in the pits and I'll be forced to sit beside my husband as the men cheer the horses on. I'll be forced to watch as Jotun gets bloodied and beaten, fighting for his life, until finally he'll die."

"You don't know that he will lose." Hannecke bites back her own tears. "Jotun's a great horse and a good fighter – he may survive."

"I would rather die myself than take the risk," I say.

And then I whisper to her, "I'm not going to get married in the morning, Hannecke. I'm going to run. I'll take Jotun and I'll go as far away as I can from here, into the high plains beyond the mountain ranges where the volcanoes spurt fire and sulphur. They won't dare to journey so far, and they'll never track us down. There are wild herds there, other horses that Jotun can run with. And who knows? Maybe I will find a forgotten tribe and make new friends. Or I will live out my life in isolation. But either way, I'll be free of them and so will Jotun. It's the only option left to me now."

I walk across the room to my bridal gown and pick up the veil. I feel the weight of the heavy lace in my hands as I walk back across the room and place it over Hannecke's head. It covers her so completely she cannot be seen.

Hannecke pushes the veil back up once more so that I can see her face and she's not crying now, she's smiling. She understands the trick we are about to perform.

"I love it!" she says to me. "You are as cunning as Loki."

Hannecke is right. My plan is the same one that the mischievous god once used long ago on the poor, stupid ogre Thrym.

"Really," I say to Hannecke, "Sigard should be thankful that I'm not marrying him off to Thor and he won't end up getting his head bashed in."

At least I'm giving him Hannecke as his bride instead of me. Sigard could do a lot worse than my best friend.

"I can't believe you're really leaving me," Hannecke says. We've been together since we were born. She's in tears now for real and so am I. We're dressed in each other's clothes and my bags are packed. Jotun is saddled and waiting. If I go now, I'll be gone before the wedding even takes place. I need to make up as much ground as I can before Sigard lifts the bridal veil.

The path I will take is along the valley to the south. I'll pass by my village on the journey, and I'll have to be careful not to be seen. If someone were to tell Steen that I'd been past, he'd know which way I'm heading. I don't want him to have the chance to track me down. The safest thing for me is to stick to the forest that skirts the edge of my village until I'm past the lake and then head for the coast from there.

This is my plan, but as I get close to my home I feel myself waver. I see the thatched tops of the longhouses and I think maybe I can just ride a little nearer and sneak a peek. It will be the last time ever that I lay eyes on the place where I was born. When I leave this time, I'm leaving forever. I know it in my bones that I will never return.

The noises of village life are so familiar to me as I draw closer. It's a busy place, our village. I hear the sounds of the forge; the blacksmith, Haur, is pumping at his bellows and there's a heavy clank of metal as he lowers the cauldron to heat the bronze. Gunnar, the ship-builder, is hammering away too, bending beams of timber to his will to construct longboats.

The children run through the streets playfighting, chasing each other armed with shields and wooden swords. Their mothers don't seem to mind them getting underfoot; they laugh and sing as they go about their work. I think about how my own mother loved to sing to me as she combed my hair.

This was once my life. Everything that mattered to me – my mother and my father, my chance to take the throne and rule my tribe with kindness and wisdom – it's all gone. All I have in the world now is my horse, my Jotun, and I know, even though the tears sting my cheeks, I have made the right decision. Keeping him safe and alive is worth exiling myself for.

As I turn him away, I take one last farewell glance

over my shoulder, back towards the village. And that is when the blacksmith chooses to pump his bellows so hard in the forge that the sparks and the flames fly up into the sky. I see the fire, feel it clutch at my chest, and I cannot breathe. I'm captured by it once more and the world around me blurs at the edges and I feel myself slipping away, back to my other self, leaving it all behind.

CHAPTER 12

The Bidding

I'd felt inside me how much it hurt Brunhilda as she looked one last time at her village and knew she never would return.

Now, a week later, I found that I couldn't return either. I was with Gudrun – we'd gone to the library together and lit the fire and Gudrun had cast her runes and I'd clutched at my necklace and I'd stared into the flames, waiting for the moment when I would be gone and… and nothing.

"I'm still here," I said with disappointment. Gudrun had to admit she didn't know why. "Perhaps we are too far away now from the Jonsmessa?" she pondered. "The days are growing shorter. The sun is almost normal now."

It was true. The light had rebalanced. At night it was so dark I found myself able to sleep once more. Maybe that was the problem too. In my sleep-deprived state I'd found the idea of possessing the mind, spirit and body of a Viking princess to be entirely plausible. Now, in the cold, pale light of dawn, with my wits about me, it seemed like a crazy idea. There was no more going back.

Filming was coming to an end too. I thought back to the beginning when we'd arrived in Iceland, how there was hardly any night and it had felt like the days were lasting forever and our time here was never going to end. Now, suddenly, it was all wrapping up in this final, mad rush. With time running short to get the movie finished and many scenes yet to be shot Katherine had deployed what film people call a "second unit". Instead of one crew, the movie was now split into two, so that while Katherine and the first unit worked on doing all the crucial emotional, romantic scenes with Jamisen and Anders, the second unit, which included the horse team, were assigned with Jimmy to do all the remaining stunt shots that needed finishing for the final cut.

Up until now Anders had been a part of our team

too, doing all his own stunts, but because he couldn't be in two places at once, Connor took over. He was fitted with a blond Sigard wig to double for Anders and he took his place in front of the cameras as we completed those final scenes.

It meant I didn't need to talk to Anders at work – which was fine by me. I hadn't spoken to him at all since our last scene together in the fire ring. A couple of times at breakfast he'd hurried after me calling my name. Once, at the buffet, he tried to corner me and talk about what had happened, saying he wanted to tell me "his side of things", but I had cut him dead and walked away. I didn't want to hear his excuses or his justifications. I guess I was being unfair on him because I knew a big part of why I was so angry wasn't even about him. I knew in my heart of hearts that what I'd asked him to do was impossible. I blamed Anders in a way for what the real Sigard had done to Brunhilda. They were one and the same to me somehow, and when Anders hadn't done what I'd wanted that day, I felt it as keenly as Brunhilda had when Sigard had betrayed her. Anyway, as far as I was concerned, I was happy never to see Anders Mortenson ever again.

Ollie, however, didn't feel the same way.

"He's been off his feed ever since Anders stopped turning up at the yard," Niamh told me. "I'm really worried about him."

It was true: Ollie did seem to miss Anders. He barely ate, picking at the oats and chaff, even when we stuck molasses in it. The shaggy goat-hair suit that we'd had sewn for him all those weeks ago had to be altered to fit his decreasing belly. Skinny and sad, his performances in front of the cameras lacked the old charisma. Instead of striding forward as Ollie had done when Anders was on his back, knees high in the air and neck arched so that his enormous mane cascaded along his crest, now he just sort of loped along like a large, sad pony. Jimmy didn't really notice the difference. He knew nothing about horses and couldn't tell a tölt from a trot, so he didn't grasp why Ollie's presence was suddenly so flat. But for those of us on the horse team, it was disheartening to see him like this. And for the filming of the final battle scene, we knew we were in trouble.

One of the scenes we had yet to shoot was a crucial moment between Ollie and Anders that would happen right near the end of the movie. It was a scene where Prince Sigard was fighting his way to reach "sleeping"

Brunhilda. Battling his way through the Viking horde to be at her side, he's outnumbered and overwhelmed by his enemy, and although he escapes, he's wounded and falls from his horse into an icy stream. Sigard is going to die right there in the water, except his beloved stallion drags him to the shore and wakes him up, saving the day so that the prince can ride on and rescue Brunhilda.

This was a crucial scene between the prince and his horse and Anders had rehearsed it many times with Ollie. He'd worn a wetsuit then because he had to fall off on purpose time and again – down into the icy stream where he'd lie, freezing cold, until Ollie came and dragged him by the collar and licked his face to wake him up and bring him back to life.

Now, with Connor in front of the cameras at the eleventh hour replacing Anders in the role of Sigard, the stunt just wasn't working. Every time he fell from Ollie's back into the frozen water, the horse would just gallop away and leave him there.

Everyone could see it wasn't going to happen. And it was Connor who called it first as he dragged himself shivering out of the stream for the eighth time that morning, his face blue with almost-hypothermia. "We're never going to get the take like this in a million years. That horse hates me! He's not responding to any of my cues. We need Anders back. I'm not falling off into that stream again for nothing!"

Jimmy put in the call to Lizzie. The first unit was busy that day filming with Anders, but Lizzie moved heaven and earth to free him up the following day so that, the next morning, Anders turned up on our set instead and we re-shot the river scene.

The look on Ollie's face when he saw that it was Anders under the blond wig that day instead of Connor is something I'll never forget. The black stallion pricked his ears forward and he gave this neigh that was like a bellow. It was so touching to see Ollie gallop over and then Anders with his arms around the stallion whispering into his ear. I have to admit I softened at that moment and felt bad that we weren't friends any more, because any boy who could affect a horse like that – who could win its trust and love like Anders Mortenson – had to be a decent person.

"Let's move on this!" Jimmy called everyone into position. "We've got Anders for the morning. We need to get the scene in the bag."

It was breathtaking to see Ollie perform that day.

He was like a different horse. The stallion seemed to have grown in stature, he stood so tall and proud with Anders on his back when they mocked up the battle scenes; and when Anders fell into the water, at the crucial moment he didn't bolt away as he had done when Connor had fallen. The black stallion stood knee-deep in the water and used his teeth to tug at Anders' collar, dragging him to shore. Then, in a moment that would be heartbreaking when it appeared on screen, he paced back and forth beside Anders' prone body at the water's edge, and began snorting and stamping, as if to demand that Anders should get up again. When Anders didn't lift his face, Ollie came close, stepping forward with his muzzle lowered to trace the ground until he reached Anders and then, in the most adorable way, he sniffed at him then pushed his velvet-soft nose into Anders' cheek, a gesture almost like a kiss, and then licked him gently, smooching his cheek until Anders coughed and spluttered and awoke.

The whole scene took only one take to get right and, when it was done, the crew gave Anders a standing ovation.

"I've got no idea how you did that." Connor shook

his head in disbelief as he came forward to take Ollie's reins.

Anders laughed. "There's a trick to it," he admitted. He leaned down to Connor. "Kiss my cheek."

Connor looked at him like he was a bit mad.

"No," Anders said, "I mean it. Go on, give me a kiss."

Connor shrugged at us and leaned in and gave Anders a peck on his right cheek.

"Eww!" He screwed up his face. "Gross!"

"It's honey," Anders said.

Connor smacked his lips. "So it is!"

Anders laughed. "That's how I trained him to kiss me awake. Honey on the cheek. Horses can't resist it."

"I guess you're good at faking stuff," I said.

I didn't mean to say it, but I was thinking it and it just came out. Niamh and Connor looked horrified that I'd just been so mean to Anders after he'd basically bailed us out by coming back and aceing the scene in one take. They looked at Anders, waiting to see what he'd say back.

"I'd better go," was all he said. "Ollie got pretty cold today shooting those scenes. I want to rug him up and give him his feed before I go back to the first unit to finish the afternoon."

Niamh waited until Anders had left with Ollie before she started up with me. "When are you going to cut him some slack?" she said. "I don't really know what's gone on between you two but he's said he's sorry, hasn't he?"

"It's not that simple," I replied. I could never explain to her that Anders had betrayed me and Bru, and as much as I wanted to, I wasn't sure I'd ever forgive him.

Anyway, in a few days, filming would come to an end and I'd never see Anders again. Or Niamh and Connor. What upset me the most about leaving though was Hammer. I never thought I could love a horse the way I had loved Piper. And maybe my love for Hammer wasn't exactly the same. Piper had been a sensitive, delicate kind of mare and Hammer was a totally different horse.

"What's going to happen to them," I asked Niamh, "once the filming is done?"

"I don't know," Niamh said. "We haven't had a chance to talk to Katherine about it. I mean, in most cases we bring our own horses to the production and when filming is over they just return to the farm with us. This time though, because we couldn't bring any horses into Iceland, Katherine used the production budget to buy Hammer and Ollie and the others, so it's actually the film company that owns them."

"So they'll keep them?"

Niamh shrugged. "What's a film company going to do with two Icelandic stallions?"

The answer came at breakfast the next morning.

"Look at this!" Niamh returned from the buffet with a piece of paper in her hand.

"There's a stack of these flyers up there," she said, shoving it across the table to me. "They're having an auction. All the sets and props, everything that they've used for filming that they don't need to hang on to, is being auctioned off. They're holding the auction in Thing-Vellir on the rock."

I didn't get the significance at first. Why did we care if they were selling off the swords and chain mail? But then I read down the list on the flyer and I saw them there in among the auction lots. They didn't even call them by their names. It just listed them as lots number 141 and 142 – Icelandic stallion (black) and Icelandic stallion (red mane).

"They're selling Hammer and Ollie? They're living creatures!" I was stunned.

Mum wasn't. "As far as the film studio is concerned, they're assets that they have no use for any more," she said, looking at the auction list. "And," she added, "to be fair, horses get sold at auction all the time. It's not that extraordinary."

Niamh was reading down the list. There were other horses on there too. Over a dozen of them that had been bought for filming.

"Connor is gonna love this," she said. "If the price is right and we can afford to ship them home, he'll want to buy them all."

I wish I could have been generous at that moment and been happy that Niamh wanted to buy the horses. I mean, she and Connor and Mark were amazing horsemen, and if Hammer went to live with them I'm sure they would take such good care of him. But that didn't mean he'd be happy.

I pushed my plate away across the table. "I've got to go."

"Hilly?" Niamh called after me but I didn't turn around. I walked out of the hotel and headed down to the stables, the wind biting at my cheeks the whole way, drawing the red blood to the surface, making them rosy with the cold. All I wanted at that moment was to be with Hammer. I was heading for his stall when I heard my name being called.

"Hilly!"

It was my mum. The insistence of her tone stopped me in my tracks. I turned to see her striding after me.

"That was very dramatic, the way you stomped out." She was puffing from running to catch me up, her breath making steam in the air. "I think you've been spending too much time with actors."

"I'm sorry…" I began but she stopped me.

"It's OK," she said. "I get why you're upset. But next time, instead of storming off, let's discuss it, OK? Sometimes these things that you think are a problem, they can wind up working out for the best."

I felt the tears welling up now and I felt stupid too. "I know," I said, "I should be happy that Hammer could end up living with Niamh and Connor, and I can always go and visit him and…"

"No, no…" Mum shook her head. "You're getting the wrong end of any number of sticks here. I'm not saying that at all. Niamh isn't buying Hammer. She's buying the rest of the horses – if the price is right. She agrees that Hammer would be better off with you. *We're* going to buy him."

I couldn't believe what I was hearing.

"What? But do we have enough money? And how would we get him home?"

Mum smiled. "On a plane, just like us – well, maybe not the same one as us – I think you have to use a cargo jet. Niamh says she has a freight company they use. They ship horses all the time back and forth in Europe. It's not as expensive as you'd think. A bit more for a long haul back to New Zealand, I guess, but if the price is right at auction, we can stretch to it…"

"You mean you're going to buy him for me?"

"Well, I have to double-check with your dad, but I'm sure he'll be OK with it." Mum shoved the flyer that she'd been clutching into my cold hand and enclosed it in her own. She looked excited. "Break open your piggy bank, Hilly. We're bidding on lot 142."

Over the following days, as filming came to an end, there was a lightness to the mood on set and this sense we were all about to go on holiday. The wrap party was held out at Blue Lagoon, the same place we'd been when we first landed here, and this time the film company booked out the whole place for the party, so we had this enormous natural hot pool all to ourselves and everything was free to eat and drink, without even the wristbands. The next day a whole bunch of the cast and crew, including Anders and Jam O'Brien, all went snowmobiling up the volcano. Mum said I should go too, but I wouldn't have enjoyed it. All I could think about now was the auction and Hammer. Mum had set a maximum price of 4,000 US dollars. She figured that it would cost us another 10,000 to fly him home to New Zealand. She'd spoken to Dad and they'd agreed between them that this was the limit. It was a lot of money, but it wasn't much for this kind of horse and I knew it. Then again, Niamh had agreed to back out of the bidding, and who else on the crew would possibly want an Icelandic stallion? So things were looking positive and Mum was doing what she did best, going into work mode and focusing on the logistics of getting Hammer back to New Zealand if we did manage to get him at auction. She'd contacted the airlines and got costings on flights, and found out about other details like quarantine at the other end. I thought he might have to be quarantined for months, but it turned out it was only a couple of weeks and there was a place that did it which was not that far from the airport, and the international horse shipping company would handle all of that. He would have to go in a cargo plane. There'd be other horses on board and a vet to care for them.

"He could be back in time for you to start training for the new season," Mum said.

I wasn't sure exactly what we'd be training for. I'd always been an eventer – and I didn't even know if Hammer could jump. Still, after being super competitive for years with Piper, I didn't even really care about the whole competition thing any more. I just wanted Hammer to be there, that was all. I wanted him to neigh to me and come running across the paddocks at home, just like he'd done here in Iceland. There's a beach near our home in Wellington where you can ride the horses and all I could think of was getting Hammer back there and riding for hours, tölting through the waves along the coast with the wind whipping at his mane, and that smooth feeling, like I was gliding on air, as we got faster and faster and I could see his knees rising up above the surf as his strides grew more powerful. I didn't care any more about bringing rosettes home for my wall. I was done with that. It would be him and me together and that was all that mattered.

Gudrun had disappeared since filming had finished. She hadn't come to the wrap party or gone snowmobiling. I think the rest of the crew thought she was just sulking because Katherine hadn't done what she'd wanted towards the end – clearly, her days of holding up the production to throw the runes or do her chanting had come to an end. But I knew it wasn't that. There was nobody on this movie with purer motives than Gudrun. She had just wanted Brunhilda's memory to be preserved in the right way.

I'd gone to her room a few times but if she was in she hadn't answered the door. She was never at breakfast or in the library. I wanted to tell her about my plan to buy Hammer, thinking that maybe that would cheer her up. But would it? If I bought Hammer and took him back to New Zealand with me, then he'd never be allowed back in Iceland again, and I wasn't sure that Gudrun would support the idea of taking one of Iceland's most amazing horses out of his homeland forever.

The auction was in the afternoon at Thing-Vellir.

"It's going to be cold standing around for hours

waiting for them to get to him, so wear a big coat," Mum warned me as we dressed ready to go over.

Niamh and Connor were already there. Some of the swords that were among the early lots were of interest to them as props, so they'd wanted to make sure they were there when the bidding began.

By the time Mum and I arrived there was a big crowd. I'd thought it would just be cast and crew. It hadn't occurred to me that locals would come along too. Thing-Vellir was in the middle of nowhere – it wasn't like there were loads of people living close by – but there were at least a dozen people in the crowd that I didn't recognise at all, so now I started worrying. What if they were local horse farmers? Or they had riding schools? There were loads of riding schools in Iceland. They'd want to buy Hammer. I felt sick as the auction numbers moved onwards. Thirty-two... sixty-four... ninety-three...

By the time we'd hit the hundred mark a few of the strangers had gone. I think they were just interested in memorabilia and furniture. But there were still a few people in the crowd that I didn't know and, as the bidding worked swiftly through the 100s, and then the 110s, and then the 120s and 130s, I genuinely thought

I was going to throw up with nerves. When lot number 139 came up and I realised it was just one more item before Ollie and then after him we'd be bidding on Hammer, I thrust my bidding number into Mum's hands.

"Will you do it?" I asked her. I was terrified of the idea of doing it now, of sticking my hand up at the wrong moment or doing it wrong and losing him.

Mum took the number on the stick and waggled it cheekily at me. "Here we go," she said. "Hammer time!"

Ollie was up first. The bidding on him started slowly. Niamh, who was standing near us with Connor and Mark flanking her on either side, was doing the bidding for them. She had this really cool way of just flicking her number up casually instead of raising her whole hand – she was really chilled out about it. Later she would tell me that her heart was pounding so hard she could hardly breathe and she wasn't cool about it at all! She sure had me fooled though as the bidding for Ollie climbed, up to $1,000, then $1,500, then up by a hundred dollars at a time and then fifty dollars until it had reached $3,850, then $3,900… $3,950… I looked at Niamh, watching for that finger to twitch and raise the price to $4,000 but I knew that she and Connor and Mark had made up a list of the horses with a top bid price on all of them, and to her this was nothing but business. They'd already bought seven horses this morning – all of them for under $2,000. Nearly $4,000 for Ollie was top dollar.

"Four thousand!" The voice wasn't Niamh's, it was a woman in the crowd I'd never seen before. She was on the phone to someone and as she spoke intently she raised her hand and shouted out to the auctioneer.

"Who is she bidding for?" Niamh hissed. "She didn't bid on any of the other horses! Where did she come from?"

"I don't know," I said.

"Four thousand one hundred!"

The bid this time was with a horse farmer, and suddenly it was all on and there were bids bouncing off the walls and the price was going up and up. Niamh threw in one last futile bid at $4,500 but she was outdone by the farmer at $4,700 and then the woman with the phone in her hand, who got Ollie for $4,800.

If I had felt sick before, I felt double-sick now.

Leave. I found myself willing it as I stared at the woman. *You've got your stallion. You've got what you came for, now go! The next horse is mine. By Odin, I command you to go.*

I saw the auctioneer's assistant scurry over to take the woman's details and she looked around towards the door. For a moment I thought my invocation of the gods had actually worked and she was about to leave. But then the phone in her hand rang again and she answered it, and frowned and nodded. Then she took the auction run sheet back out of her pocket and held the phone to her ear and stayed facing the podium. She wasn't done yet.

"Lot 142," the auctioneer chanted, "lot 142, 142, the last of the equines up for bidding on today, and this one is a stallion with a red mane... Can we start the bidding at $3,000? Who'll give me $3,000?"

I looked at Mum. Why wasn't she raising her hand?

"Calm down," Mum whispered to me. "It's early days, we need to flush out who else is bidding."

"But what if no one..."

My protest got immediately crushed by the sound of a man's voice. "Three thousand!" It was the horse farmer, arms folded. He used the nod of his head to signal his interest.

"Three two!"

The bid was with Mum! We were in! We were doing this! We were bidding on Hammer!

"Three three!" the farmer came back confidently.

"Three four." Mum's voice, cool and confident.

"We're at $3,400," the auctioneer recapped. "Do we have $3,500?"

Her question hung unanswered in the air. Nothing. My heart was hammering in my ears. We had him! We had him for $3,400! Six hundred to spare and...

"Three four fifty," the farmer came back.

"Three five." Mum didn't pause. She was trying to crush him out of the game, make him see that she was unbeatable, but I knew we were close to our limit now. Only $500 to go.

The air was heavy with anticipation. Mum looked straight ahead, refusing to engage with the other bidder, her eyes confidently locked on the auctioneer.

"Three five fifty," the farmer said.

"Three six." Mum, again, quick, decisive.

The farmer unfolded his arms, jammed his hands in his pockets.

"How about it, sir?" The auctioneer turned her gaze to him. "Let's finish this, shall we? Three seven?"

The farmer stood motionless, his face blank.

"We have the bid with the woman to my left at three thousand six hundred," the auctioneer called. "Going once, going twice…"

"Four thousand!"

It was the woman on the phone! The one who'd bought Ollie. She was still here and she was bidding. And in one single call she had reached our top bid.

"Mum?" I felt my chest tighten, like I could hardly breathe. We'd already settled this though – $4,000 was the limit. I knew that.

Mum looked at the auctioneer, and then Gudrun was suddenly at my shoulder and pressing my arm. She gave me a wink. "Four thousand one hundred."

We were still bidding! I couldn't believe it!

"Four two."

"Four three."

"Four four."

The bid was back with the woman on the phone. My heart was racing. We were already $400 over our maximum bid, but I could see the look on Mum's face and on Gudrun's. Both of them had disliked each other during this film, but I knew they had one thing in common. They both hated to lose.

"Four five." Mum's voice.

"Four six." The farmer! He was still in the bidding!

"Four seven." Gudrun this time, clutching my arm.

"Four eight." The farmer.

"Four nine." Gudrun again.

The bid was back with us. We were almost $1,000 over our limit.

"The bid is with the ladies on my left at $4,900," the auctioneer said. He looked to the farmer, who raised his finger.

"I have $5,000."

I felt sick.

"Are you coming back to us?" the auctioneer asked. "Are you still in the running for lot number 142? Going once…"

"Do it," Gudrun encouraged to my mother. "We can go to $5,100…"

But the auctioneer wasn't talking to us any more. His gaze had swept across to the woman. She held one hand aloft to him in what I hoped was a signal that she was dropping out, but then I realised she'd raised her phone so her caller could hear as she shouted out the bid.

"Six thousand dollars."

And in that moment I knew nobody would beat her. Hammer was gone.

CHAPTER 13

Fire Stallion

For ages after the auction, Mum and Gudrun and I talked about whether we could have done things differently. Would the farmer have outbid us again if we'd raised?

"It wouldn't have mattered in the end what he did," Mum said. "It was that woman. She was going to win at any cost and she had deep pockets."

"There's no way the pockets were hers." Gudrun shook her head. "The question is, who was on the other end of that phone? She was bidding on behalf of someone else."

We asked around the crew at dinner that night but nobody knew the woman or who she'd been bidding for. She'd bought just the two horses that day, Ollie and Hammer. Niamh and Connor were booked on a flight back to Ireland with their seven horses, and when Niamh came to dinner that night she had news from the freight company.

"Ollie and Hammer are on the same airline as my boys but it's a different flight. They're leaving tomorrow," Niamh told us, "flying direct out of Reykjavik to the States."

"Do you have more details? Where are they going?"

"Transiting through LA." Niamh shrugged. "That's all I could find out. I'm sorry, Hilly. They're not my horses. I was lucky the shipping company told me that much."

I still couldn't believe we hadn't won. I know Mum was right – even if we'd had another thousand to bid, maybe even if we'd had another ten, that woman wasn't ever going to lose. I kept having flashbacks to the auction, the way she'd stood there all cool, full of confidence when she flicked up her bidder's paddle, the smugness of her smile when she gave the auctioneer's assistant her details afterwards, as if she knew all along she would be the victor.

After Piper had died, I'd been left with this hollow feeling, an overwhelming sense of loneliness. My grief at losing Hammer hurt the same way. I realised now that in my mind I'd believed he was already mine to take home. I'd had it all planned, how he'd come to live in New Zealand with me. It had never occurred to me that we might not win. We were meant to be together.

That evening after dinner it began snowing. It wasn't heavy snow, just a swirl of white flakes in the black night air, kissing sharp at my cheeks as I walked alone to the stables. Niamh said the transporter was turning up tomorrow. Hammer would be loaded onto the lorry and driven through the bleak moonscape that led to Keflavik airport and put on board the carrier flight. And then he'd be gone from me forever.

All we had left, he and I, was the next few hours, and I wanted us to be together for all of them.

Hammer had his head out over the loose box door to greet me as he always did. My heart stopped for a moment as I entered the stables when I caught sight of the beauty of his face for what would be the last time.

"Hammer, I'm so sorry. I tried, truly I did. I wanted so much for you to be mine…"

My horse craned his neck out over the door of the

stall and gave a stamp to signal his impatience. He couldn't understand why I held back from him. Why was it taking me so long to approach him when usually I would rush to his side?

I could see the hot steam of his breath in the cold night air. Would it be cold where he was going? Would his new owners love him as much as I had loved him?

He stamped again, a little cross this time at my continuing to keep my distance. He peered out at my with those sweet, inquisitive blackberry eyes peeking from beneath that long forelock. Then he waggled his head from side to side, encouraging me to step up so that we could begin the game.

"OK, OK." I came to him and stood in front of him on the other side of the loose box door. Hammer dropped his forehead to meet mine and then he began ducking and weaving his muzzle back and forth. Peek-a-boo, and then, when I started crying and I wouldn't keep playing, he began nudging me with his nose as if to say, "Hey, this is our game. Why are you sad? What's wrong?"

That was when I started bawling. The hot tears stung my frozen cheeks. Hammer kissed my cold, damp skin with his warm muzzle and I fell against him and grasped his mane and buried my face deep into it.

"I'm so sorry! I wanted you to be mine forever…"

I was lost in the tangle of the fiery strands of brilliant red and gold. And suddenly, like the swirl of the snowflakes in the night air, the world was spiralling around me. I could smell the burning sage and hear the crackle of the flames as they sparked and burst into glowing runes. The Cross-Over was happening once more. The fire that had brought me to Brunhilda before was with me again. It was in the stallion himself, in the fire of his mane, and as I held him tight in the darkness and muttered his true name, "Mjölnir…" I felt the world slipping away and soon I wasn't there in the stables any more. I was on the barren icy plains beyond the lakes and mountains of Thing-Vellir. Ahead of me stretched the bleak, desolate coast of the south, and I was tölting hard against the wind. The sword swung at my hip as, beneath me, Jotun was striding like a giant – the two of us, running together to the end of the earth.

CHAPTER 14

Long Shadows

I have never been this far from home before. The land is different here, vast and empty, the wind so brutal that the birch trees never grow taller than spindly saplings. To the right of me is the sea and to the left stands the great volcano Eyjafjallajökull, the glacial giant. Eyjafjallajökull is snow-covered now because he's sleeping but he's not dead. My father always said there will be a time again when Eyjafjallajökull will awaken with a rumble that shakes the ground and darkens the skies, and his deep, blood-red throat will swell with pure fire that oozes out, destroying everything in its path all the way to the sea so that, when it's done, all that is left is black ash.

I do not fear the volcano as I ride in its long shadow.

It shows no signs of awakening and the ground slumbers peacefully beneath Jotun's hooves as we tölt on, as fast as we can into the hard headwind that blows in off the coast. Once we are past the domain of Eyjafjallajökull, I will change direction and go inland, cutting through the valleys, taking that river vein between mountains where the waterfalls on either side have frozen solid so that the cliff faces hang with blue icicles.

The early winter cold grips the land here and the ponds are all frozen over too. I stopped earlier and tried to break the ice with my sword so that my horse could take a drink but it was too thick. Jotun will stay thirsty until we reach the river that I see emerging between the mountains in the distance, the blue water making tentacles between the ice floes and straw-coloured tussock mounds. The river spreads out wide in parts and looks deep. We'll need to be careful when we reach it to choose our point to cross or we'll end up in it all the way up to our necks. If Jotun and I get wet in this freezing cold wind, we won't last long.

We'll follow the river heading into the mountains, going inland where the birch trees grow tall, not like the little scrubby bushes that barely dare to poke their faces above the black earth here. I'm going to build myself a house from those birch trees. Steen and I did it once when we were children – we built a playhouse using skinny twiglets we'd found on the forest floor, basket-woven together around four corner posts to create our walls. We thatched the roof with tussock grass. I remember that as soon as it was built Steen refused to let me play in it with him, even though I had done most of the work myself. So nothing has changed really. But this new house that I will build for myself won't be a game. It will be a longhouse, like the one I grew up in, and I will craft it myself with my axe and the boughs of trees, and there will be a firepit at the heart of it. I will keep a flame lit in the long, dark evenings and cook whatever I hunt – hares, probably – and use their skins to make my bed. Jotun will not sleep inside with me – he likes it outdoors. He will love the mountain grass in our new home – high country grass is very sweet. And there will be other horses there too, wild herds. He will get to know them, slowly at first, making friends. He'll start at the bottom, as a newcomer to a herd usually does, but he'll work his way up. He will rule them in the end. My horse is a natural leader. So at least, in this way, one of us will get to rule.

Did I do the right thing to run? I had no choice. I would

have stayed and fought, but I would have lost, and then Jotun would have had no protector. This was the only way, and as I put more and more distance between myself and my old village, the things that I leave behind bother me less and less. I have everything that I truly love in the world right here beneath me. I have my horse.

We tölt on, Jotun boldly striding out over the rough terrain. It seems like we've been going forever across this bleak windswept land, but now at last the mouth of the river comes clearly into view. The water is half-frozen. In places it flows smoothly and in others it forms ice floes that clog the arterial routes, pushing the water in different directions into the tussock grass and through the marshes, grasslands and stones, ice and water all braided together as the river does its best to flow down to the sea.

I am thinking about the best way to pick our path across this complicated terrain (without getting a leg trapped in the thick drifts of ice or ending up being submerged too deep in the river's flow) when I hear my name being called.

Brunhilda! Brunhilda!

At first I think I must be imagining it. I'm all alone out

here in the middle of nowhere. Who calls my name in this desolate place?

And then I turn round and I see the rider coming after me and my heart lurches.

It is Sigard.

Honestly, why does he call to me? As if I would run to his arms! Doesn't he know he's the one I'm running from?

I cluck Jotun on into a pace now and I feel him shift his legs and throw himself forward, and suddenly he's striding completely differently, his two legs on each side of his body moving in unison as pairs. We are moving swiftly now, but the ground here is rough, too rough to maintain this speed, and we are approaching the river's edge. To try to bowl on into the water without taking the time to navigate a path is too risky. And Sigard is right behind me, matching our speed stride for stride.

So, I have a choice. Push Jotun on, leap into the river, risk the ice floes and the torrent, and the freezing cold of soaking wet furs, and swim for it, make it to the other side and hope Sigard is too afraid to follow. Or make my stand against him here and now, hold my ground, turn and face him.

When I ran away from Thing-Vellir it was to keep Jotun safe. I was never afraid of Sigard and I'm not afraid of him now. If he has come all this way to confront me – well, it would be a shame to disappoint him.

"Ho, Jotun!" I sit up in the saddle and give the reins the lightest check and I feel my horse respond and come back to me.

"See? We've got company," I tell him. "Be ready and have your wits about you."

The mare that Sigard rides is one of my father's own herd. I recognise her instantly. Her name is Hrönd, a pretty mouse-grey dun with a charcoal mane. Jotun knows her too. He gives her a clarion call, whinnying his greeting to her. At least some of us are pleased to see each other.

Sigard pulls to a halt a few horse lengths from us. Hrönd stamps and frets as he holds her back, keeping distance between us as he once again shouts my name: "Brunhilda!" His voice is almost lost in the wind. "I've come to bring you home."

I laugh. "Because you have realised you love me and you cannot live without me?"

Sigard's face darkens. "Love you? Right now I can't think of anyone in the kingdoms of Iceland or Greenland that I hate more. You made me look a fool."

247

"You made yourself a fool when you sided with my brother."

Sigard loses his temper when I say this and gives a vicious yank on the reins, so that poor Hrönd snorts in shock and rears up.

"Watching you being cruel to your horse only makes me gladder than ever that I left you at the altar," I tell him.

Sigard snarls. "Do you know, before I came to Iceland, everyone told me you were beautiful, but nobody mentioned your stubborn and obstinate nature."

"I'm sorry I'm such a disappointment." I pull a face at him. "I'm sure there are lots of nice girls back in Greenland who'll want to be your princess and who have far better qualities than I."

"I'm sure there are," Sigard agrees. "But I chose you as my wife and I told everybody I was bringing a princess back with me. It shames my honour if you do not return with me in my longboat, and I couldn't bear that. So you will come. Kicking and screaming for all I care, but you will come. We're going to return to Thing-Vellir and we will forget this little outburst you've had and everything will be as it was meant to be. There will be feasts and horse fights and we'll start our life together."

Sigard stretches out a gloved hand, inviting me to take it.

I stare at the hand, dumbfounded at his arrogance. Then I raise my own hand and reach to my hip and unsheathe my sword. Sunlight strikes the steel as I raise my weapon.

"Let me go, Sigard," I say to him. "I'm asking nicely but I will not ask again."

Sigard laughs. "You really want to take me on?"

I'm not laughing. "Draw your sword or I'll run you through unarmed," I reply.

Sigard reaches to his hip and unsheathes his blade. Hrönd snorts uneasily beneath him as he tightens his legs around her, readying himself. Sigard circles the blade above his head, which looks very threatening and glamorous but it's a waste of energy. He's such a show-off. My father was a clever fighter but he never did unnecessarily fancy moves. "In a fight, don't ever think about looking pretty," he once told me. "Be effective. Make every move count. Focus on one thing only – delivering the killing blow."

Sigard begins spinning his blade, like he's performing for an audience. But there's no one here to applaud him except the ravens wheeling above. And if he thinks I will wait for him to finish off his shiny tricks before I strike, he's wrong.

"Aargh!" The guttural scream comes out of me instinctively as I kick Jotun on and ride straight for my foe with my sword thrust out at my hip. Sigard has no chance to do anything more than parry the blow, but I'm expecting that and already I've turned Jotun and I'm striking at Sigard again and again, swinging the blade. I hack at him and the second blow finds his ribs. He doubles over in pain, yanks at the reins and spins Hrönd away from me to give himself time to regroup.

"You witch!"

I have bruised him but his chain mail stopped the blade from piercing.

"Next time I'll make you bleed," I warn Sigard.

Jotun's eyes are blazing at our enemy. My stallion dances underneath me, snorting and fretting against the bit as he plunges up and down on the spot, keen to attack. I have to hold him back.

"You got lucky." Sigard swings his sword once more in a fanciful, extravagant gesture. "You won't get lucky again."

"Steady, my friend," I whisper to Jotun. "Wait for it..."

We must think like our enemy to be victorious. Sigard

fights with the bluster of a showman so his next move is bound to be a dramatic strike. Let the sword swirl. All we have to do is wait for him to expose himself and...

There! His sword goes up again above his head and this time I see the vulnerable point in the armpit of his chain mail. Instead of using my sword I reach for the axe on my back. I can't get close enough to swing at this range and so I throw the axe instead, launching it through the air. The axe head pierces his chain mail and Sigard lets out a cry of pain and falls from Hrönd to the ground. I expect him to get up again but he stays on the tussock grass where he fell, clutching his shoulder where the axe struck him and groaning with pain. I dismount from Jotun's back and, holding my sword outstretched in front of me, I walk over to stand above him. I put the point of my blade to the groove of his throat.

"Go on then!" Sigard pants out the words. "Finish me!"

I shake my head. "No," I say. "I'm not going to kill you, Sigard. I'm letting you go. But you must give me your word that you'll leave this place once and for all. Go back to Greenland. This ends now. Do we have a deal?"

I prod Sigard with my sword and he reluctantly nods

in agreement. I put out my hand and feel him clasp his fingers around my wrist, but instead of letting me pull him to his feet, he yanks suddenly and drags me down to the ground. He's much heavier than me, stronger too, and he wrestles me onto my back and sits on me so that he straddles me, crushing the air from my lungs.

"You should know by now not to trust me," he says as he unsheathes his dagger.

I never trusted Sigard, but I did have faith in my horse.

Jotun rears above us, blocking out the sun. I see his front hooves thrash through the sky and then, with one swift and deadly blow, he strikes at Sigard.

Sigard still has the dagger in his hand as he slumps forward on top of me. I feel a sharp pain in my gut as he collapses. Struggling against his weight I push him off, rolling sideways, getting on all fours on the ground, gasping for air.

Sigard is lying motionless on the ground. I prod him with my sword. He doesn't move. There's a trickle of blood on his skull where Jotun struck him.

I look down at my hands and see blood on them too, so I wipe them against my fur coat. Then I raise them again to my face, but now they are worse. There's even more blood.

I look down and I see this damp, red stain seeping through the furs, spreading at my gut. This blood, it isn't Sigard's at all, it's my own. His dagger must have struck me when he collapsed on top of me.

"Jotun?" I feel faint all of a sudden. The horizon begins moving up and down. My vision blurs. I stagger backwards, collapse to my knees.

My stallion gives a worried snort and comes to me where I kneel in the tussock grass. He nudges me with his muzzle as if to say, "Get up! We've just won! Now let's go!"

I take hold of his mane with a grunt, and pull myself up to my feet again. I walk over to Hrönd, who waits patiently at her dead master's side. I unbridle her and slip off her saddle so that she's free to go. Then I make my way to Jotun. He's stamping his hooves, impatient for me to mount up again. The world is spinning. I can feel the blood seeping warm at my belly but I'm so cold now. I steady myself against Jotun's shoulder and then I take his saddle off too, and slip his bridle from his head.

"We don't need these things any more," I whisper to him. "I'm going to ride you without them from now on."

My fingers snake through his ropey mane. With the last of my strength I grasp on tight and pull myself up onto his back so that I'm bareback and controlling him with my hands on his neck and my legs around him to steer him and move him on.

I look across the tussock plains, back in the direction we've just come. If we ride as the raven flies we might reach my village by nightfall. I can go back to my longhouse and Hannecke can tend my wound, feed me, keep me warm and help me recover. But what then? If I return, then I accept that Steen will be my king and my brother will make me pay for leaving him – and for Sigard's death. Steen is dumb but he's smart when it comes to finding the best way to hurt me. He'll take Jotun from me for sure and use my horse as sport in the stallion pits.

I put my hand to my stomach and I feel the blood, hot and pulsing against my freezing cold fingers. And I know I have no choice.

Steeling myself, I pick up the reins and I turn my horse.

Not for home, not for the village, but onwards towards the river. I'm not going home. And neither is he. We're carrying on.

We cross the river and make it safely to the other side before following the valley between the mountains. Waterfalls spill down from the cliffs above us, cascades of blue water and icicles. The sky is darkening and, as night closes in, the stars are spread like a blanket against the blackness above us and the night air takes on a strange green glow. The Northern Lights will come tonight. They will light up the sky like an emerald fire above us. They will be the last thing I see as I slump forward on Jotun's mighty shoulders and then fall down to the ground. I have lost so much blood my body is a feather as I fall. Yet despite my lightness, I cannot move at all. The last of my strength has been drained from me.

There's no pain. As I lie there with the last of my warmth ebbing from me I don't feel at all cold. "Jotun." My eyes close, but I sense that he's there, right beside me. I want to say goodbye to him, to tell him that in my whole life I loved him above all else and that everything, all of this, was worth it because he's safe and now he's free. I hope he knows these things. I hope he knows how much I love him because I find that the cold has made my lips too numb to form the words. I can feel his warm breath on my cheek as the snow falls and dusts my skin, and as I lie there I don't feel even the slightest bit scared. The greatest of all the gods, Odin, he chooses your time to die. And now I'm here and he has chosen mine.

CHAPTER 15

Casting the Runes

To come back into your own world is a shock, but to be wrenched back from the brink of death is like nothing I could ever describe. I remember how Gudrun found me in the stables that night, curled up and heaving my grief on the straw. She said I was speaking, babbling to myself, but the words made no sense at all.

"It was Icelandic, the tongue you spoke," Gudrun said, "but such an ancient form of the language that not even I could interpret it. Anyway, you were so upset, I couldn't make out what you were saying."

I don't remember my words either, but I remember Gudrun's as she crouched there beside me, telling me to breathe, to calm down. She was trying to get me to stop crying, but I couldn't. I was sobbing so hard.

I must have been a sight, face smeared with tears, shaking and shivering. Gudrun stayed with me, protecting me, clutching me tight as she rocked me in her arms. "Shush, shush, I understand," she cooed, "I know it's so hard to say goodbye. You will miss him so very much…"

"No!" I sobbed even harder at the horror of being misunderstood. "This is not about Hammer. It's Bru…"

I lost my voice again to the sobbing.

"Bru? So you went back again?" Gudrun was confused. "But how? The fire, it didn't work any more. How did you do it?"

"Hammer's mane," I sobbed. "I put my hands in it and it took me to her. She was running away. She wanted to save Jotun from the pits but Sigard came after her, he wouldn't let her go. They fought…"

"And Sigard beat her?" Gudrun asked.

"No! She won but when she showed him mercy Sigard attacked her like a coward. He got on top of her and was going to kill her, but Jotun fought back – he struck him down to save her. Except Sigard had a knife and it must have pierced her stomach. Oh, Gudrun! It was awful…"

"Are you sure she died though?" Gudrun couldn't quite believe it. "Perhaps he just wounded her?"

I started sobbing again, so hard this time I found it impossible to breathe and get the words out.

"Shhh." Gudrun held me tighter. "You're hyperventilating. Take deep breaths. Calm down."

"You don't understand," I panted. "I wasn't just there. I was *her*! I felt it, all of it! I died with her!"

I could still feel the stab in my gut, and the warmth as the blood seeped out, soaking into my furs. I had been Bru and she had been me, right until the very end when I felt her ebb away, separating from me, and then I'd been whiplashed back to my own body, the Cross-Over this time like being dragged into a jet engine. I was back. I was alive. And suddenly she was gone.

For so long now our universes, our very selves, had been intertwined, and now Bru was dead. And I, I was just Hilly again. I had never felt more alone in my life than I did on that stable floor that night.

"I don't understand." I looked up at Gudrun, my eyes blurred with tears. "She was supposed to be queen. The legend says so. The runes predicted it."

"The runes are not infallible," Gudrun said. "They

can be hard to interpret. It's possible I misread their meaning. Brunhilda was supposed to marry Sigard and be his queen. And her wedding did take place – except Hannecke was there in her stead. Their marriage would have been binding on the Law Rock, so perhaps Hannecke remained queen in Bru's name?"

"I hope that's true," I said. "Bru would have liked that."

Gudrun helped me to my feet. "Are you OK?" she asked.

I shook my head. "I don't know… I just feel like I've failed her. I couldn't stop her from dying and I couldn't even make Katherine tell the truth about her and Sigard, about how strong she really was. She should have been the hero, not him."

Gudrun took me by the shoulders and held me so that we were face to face. She looked very serious.

"Listen to me, Hilly. I'm the one who has failed, the one who's guilty here. You were dragged into this by me. I never told you what I was doing, and what I needed you for. And yet, when I called upon you, when Brunhilda needed you, you never once hesitated. You fought for her all the way and are braver than you realise. So, yes, you are right, we did not win this time, not completely anyway. But your courage and your love for her changed the course of the movie. It might not have changed the ending, but her strength will show through on the screen. Don't think that this is the end. Your journey, the saga, is far from over. Take what you have learned here and use it to tell your own stories now. Make them honest and powerful and true. Live a life that matters, Hilly, and in that way you will honour the spirit of Brunhilda. That's what she would have wanted for you."

"I will," I replied through my tears, "I promise that. To her, and to you."

The school term started the same week that I got home. Suddenly I was back in my old life again and it felt like I'd never been in Iceland at all. Mum was fussing about the fact I couldn't find my socks that went with my uniform and making me a lunchbox and complaining about the state of my room, and I couldn't believe how regular and routine everything was once more.

Dad loved hearing all abut Iceland but Sarah-Kate

didn't even want to listen to my stories. Even though I was the one who'd been on the other side of the world, working like a professional on a movie, and she'd just been doing the usual stuff, she was obssessed with her own life just as always. She'd got her learner's licence while I'd been away and kept showing off about that and bossing me around, making me do the dishes when it was really her turn. I put up with it though and I didn't pick fights with her as much as I used to before. She wasn't such a bad sister. It could have been worse. I could have had a brother like Steen.

I hadn't said goodbye to Anders. He and Jam had left before the crew, flying out on a private jet, which was such a Hollywood thing to do. I told Emily and Rose in my class that I'd hung out with Anders Mortenson when I was working on the film and that we'd done stunts together, but they thought I was making it up. So they told Lianna and Kylie, who've always been total mean girls. And that was when the four of them began teasing me about it.

"You're lying," Lianna said. "I bet you've never even met him."

"I'm not," I insisted. "We really did do stunts together."

"So when the movie comes out, will you be in it?" Kylie asked.

"Yes," I said, "but you won't see that it's me because I have a wig on to make it look like I'm Jamisen O'Brien."

Kylie had laughed at this. "So you're in the movie except we can't see it's really you? OMG, you're such a liar!"

I stopped telling people after that, but it didn't matter. By then they'd spread it around the whole school and everybody was talking about me, about how I had this whole fantasy in my head that I was a film star.

Whenever I'd had trouble at school, I'd always had Piper to come home to. If I was upset I'd just get my bridle and ride bareback, hacking her along the paths from our place that led down to the beach. Without her, I felt like I had no one.

I tried to be strong, to focus on what Gudrun had said to me that night in Iceland, about being brave and fighting to become someone who mattered, but the truth was I didn't feel like I had much fight left in me any more.

"I'm not going to school," I told Mum when she

263

tried to rouse me out of bed on the Monday morning, ten days after our return to Wellington.

"Why not?" Mum asked.

"I didn't sleep much last night," I replied. "I still have jet lag. I think I need to stay home from school."

"Jet lag?" Mum raised an eyebrow. "Hilly, we've been back for nearly two weeks. Get up and stop mucking about! We leave in ten minutes. I'm going to drop you off on my way into town – and if you make me late for my meeting, I will *not* be happy about it."

I got up. You don't mess with my mum when she's in one of her moods. I think she was a bit stressed because she was having a meeting that day at Miramar about a new movie that was in production and she really wanted the job. She spent the whole car journey on the speaker phone to Nicky about it, so we didn't really talk when she was driving me to school. When we got to the school car park though, she stopped talking to Nicky at last and she turned to me. "Finding it hard to adjust to being back?"

I nodded. "I'll get used to it."

How could I be the same girl who'd spent the past two months training wild horses and doing death-defying stunts and battle scenes with swords, when now, in the so-called "real world", I spent my lunch hour hiding in a toilet cubicle to get away from the girls in my class who kept tormenting me?

When lunch time came that day I couldn't face more time in the toilet block, so I stayed back in the classroom to talk to Ms Dunningham about catching up on the assignments I'd missed out on while I'd been away.

At the end of the day though, there was no more avoiding them. Lianna and Kylie caught the same bus home as me.

They were there, waiting in a big group with a whole lot of other kids from our year. As soon as Kylie caught sight of me, she started laughing and whispering something to Lianna.

I was so busy staring at my feet, trying to ignore them, I guess I didn't see the car coming at me.

It could have killed me. Well, maybe I'm exaggerating, but it did this massive swerve right in front of me, and if I'd been walking any faster it would have got me and knocked me clean to the ground, I'm certain of it.

It was one of those fast sports cars, a fancy one with a loud engine. I don't know anything about car brands but it had a horse symbol on the bonnet, and it was black with tinted windows. Not the sort of car that you usually see in the school car park at Otaki Intermediate.

It pulled up so close to me it nearly ran over my feet and I lunged forward and slammed my hands down on the bonnet. "Hey!" I shouted. "Watch where you're going! You could kill someone driving like that!"

I know I shouldn't have done that. It was probably a really expensive car and I could have put a dent in it. But they'd nearly hit me! And I guess I was pretty angry by then anyway after the day I'd had. Being almost run over was the final straw.

The driver turned off the car engine and then the door opened. It wasn't like a regular car door – it didn't swing outwards, it raised up in the air like a bird's wing lifting to the sky, except with this super smooth, hi-tech glide to it. Between almost being run over by it and the magical doors on this thing, I was pretty sure that every single person waiting for the bus who hadn't already been looking at me by now had their eyes glued on me for sure.

And then he stepped out of the car. I didn't recognise him at first. Not because of the dark glasses. They weren't what threw me. It was the hair. The last time I'd seen him, he'd been blond with a high quiff and side braids and tattoos. Now, his hair was like it had been in the old days – short-cropped and dark. I had no idea how he'd had time to grow it back like that. Filming had only finished three weeks ago.

"Hey, Hilly." Anders Mortenson took off his sunglasses and gave me one of those sweet smiles of his. "I saw your mum at the studio this morning. She told me I'd find you here."

I stared at him, not knowing what to say.

"So..." Anders shoved his hands in his pockets. "So, umm, hi. How have you been?"

There was a disarming awkwardness about him. But then he always had been a great actor. Was he really kind of goofy and uncomfortable about meeting me again? Or was this an act he was putting on?

"I've been OK," I said. "Why are you here?" I asked, conscious of the looks that the rest of the class were giving me.

"OK, cool, cut to the chase, that's good. I've always liked that about you," Anders said. "Yeah. I'm here for a reason. I came here to see you."

"Well, now you've seen me," I said, "you can go."

"You're still angry with me," Anders said. "I figured you would be."

My bus had arrived but nobody was getting on board. On the sidewalk Lianna and Kylie and Emily and Rose and pretty much all the rest of my class were gawping at the sight of me talking with Anders Mortenson.

"I can give you a lift?" Anders countered. "We can talk in the car?"

I hesitated.

"Come on, Hilly," Anders said. "I'm not kidding. I came all this way to talk to you. Let me take you home."

The group at the bus stop was getting bigger now. It was like the whole school was watching me. Lianna had recovered from her shock at seeing Anders and now she was fixing her hair and preparing to come over and introduce herself. We needed to go.

"OK," I said. "Sure, thanks. A lift would be great."

I stepped around to the passenger side and lowered myself into the car seat. It was really close to the ground. Anders got into the driver's seat and pressed a button on the dashboard and the gull wings of the car doors lowered once more and we were locked inside together.

"What sort of car is this?" I asked him.

"Ferrari," Anders said. "It belongs to the studio. They're trying to bribe me into making this movie with them so they loaned it to me while I'm here. I just got my licence! It's kinda cool to drive, I guess – not as much fun as being on an Icelandic horse though."

He said it like he meant it, but then, like I say, he was a good actor.

He was a good driver too, just as much a natural behind the wheel of a car as he was on horseback, and as the Ferrari sped along the winding clifftop roads that led back towards my house, I wound down my window and enjoyed the feeling of the wind whipping my hair against my cheeks.

"I'm sorry that we never spoke before I left," Anders started off. "I got the feeling you didn't want to talk to me though."

"You got the feeling because I didn't," I confirmed.

"Because I wouldn't stand by you when you wanted to change the script?"

"It goes a bit deeper than that," I said.

Anders sighed. "Hilly, I get that you really cared about Brunhilda, and what happened to her. But have you ever seen a movie where they don't fall in love, where there's no happy ending? Where the hero turns out at the last minute to be the villain…"

"…and where the heroine dies?"

I finished his sentence for him.

"That's what really happened in the end," I said. "Sigard didn't marry her. He hunted her down for revenge because she wouldn't marry him and he killed her."

"Oh," Anders said. "Umm, I'm… sorry?"

I shook my head. "It's not your fault. It never was. I guess I blamed you for what he'd done to her. It's just so unfair, you know? She should have been queen."

Anders smiled. "In the movie, she gets to be queen – even if it is queen of Greenland. So maybe that's her moment, and maybe that's a good thing after all?"

I smiled back at him. "Maybe," I agreed, although it sounded a bit of a cop-out to me. "Maybe that's how she should be remembered." I looked out at the road ahead. We were winding down now, coming out the other side of the bush-clad mountain road that ran between the school and my place. "This is it up ahead," I said, pointing to the long avenue of poplar trees that led to my house and the stables nearby. "Casa Hilly."

"It's just like you described," Anders said. "I wish I could live somewhere like this instead of being in LA or New York or always on the set of a movie somewhere. It'd be nice to have my own stables and paddocks like this to keep my horse in."

"You have a horse?" I said.

"Yeah, I do," Anders said. "I bought him recently. He's a pretty cool guy. He's part of the reason I'm here."

"What do you mean?" I said. "I thought you came to apologise to me?"

"Oh, I did," Anders said. He smiled. "And to bring you a present."

"Yeah?" I turned my head over my shoulder and looked in the back seat of the car. It was empty. "So where is it?"

Anders pulled the Ferrari up in front of my house and turned off the engine. "Come and see," he said.

I stepped out of the car and he took my hand. "We need to go this way." He began to lead me away from my house, down to the stables.

"How do you know where to go?"

"I've been here all day," Anders replied, "settling them in to their new home."

"Them? New home?"

"Like I was saying in the car –" Anders smiled at me – "I don't have a place like this right now. I'm always busy with work and I move around all the time, so it's impossible for me to keep a horse. So I was wondering if you'd take him from here and keep him for me? I'd pay you, of course. Room and board, that kind of thing. I'd pay you to ride him too, if you were willing. There's no one else I'd trust to get on him. Also, you know how to tölt and I'm pretty sure no one else in New Zealand does!"

I looked at Anders. "You brought an Icelandic horse?"

"Kind of…" Anders said as we entered the yard and I saw the jet black face peering out over the stable door.

"Ollie!" I couldn't believe it. "You bought Ollie!"

"Uh-huh!" Anders smiled. "I mean, I loved him. I couldn't stand the thought of anyone having him except me. But you'll be taking care of him for me – if you agree – and I'd come and visit him. All the time. Well, as much as I can. Hopefully I'll be doing this new film right here in New Zealand so I'll be living in Wellington for a while."

I stroked Ollie's face. "I can't believe it," I said. "I never thought I'd see him again. When that woman bid on him…"

"She was working for me," Anders said. "I couldn't be there. Anyway, I wanted it to be a surprise."

"A surprise that you bought Ollie?"

"No." Anders shook his head. "Not Ollie. Your gift. I wanted to surprise you."

I felt my heart pounding in my chest. The woman that day, she'd bought two horses.

"Anders?" I could hardly speak. "Is he really here?"

Anders pointed to the loose box behind me. The doors were latched shut.

"Why don't you go and see?"

My hands were shaking as I worked the bolt on the door and swung it open.

And there he was, black eyes meeting mine and his mane like fire, flickering in the darkness.

"Hammer!"

He nickered as he came out of the shadows, running to me. I ran to him too, throwing my arms around his neck, hugging him hard, my face buried deep in his enormous mane. Hammer was making these soft little whinnies as if he were telling me all about his travels to reach me. The saga of his journey to a new world.

"It makes the whole secret bidder thing totally worth it," said Anders, watching us.

I turned round, my eyes wet with tears, and I punched him in the arm.

"Hey!" Anders was taken aback. "What's that for?"

"Because you're a real jerk for putting me through that, you know? I thought I was never going to see him again."

And then I threw myself at Anders and hugged him almost as hard as I'd just hugged Hammer. "Thank you for doing it. Thank you for buying him for me!"

"Take it easy!" Anders winced at the power of my hug. And then he hugged me back. "He was always your horse. I just brought him home, that's all."

After Anders had gone, I stayed down at the stables with Ollie and Hammer. I groomed them both, and then I lay on the floor of Hammer's stall and just stared and stared at him for ages, taking in the beauty of him, the shaggy dark coat and the lushness of his fire-coloured mane. He was mine now. *My horse. My horse.* I kept saying the words to myself. I really couldn't believe it. It was like in that one moment everything had changed. My life was different now. I had my horse back with me, plus I had Ollie, and Anders and I were friends again.

In the weeks to come, as we hacked the horses out together, riding into the hills and down to the beach,

I would share the whole story with Anders, about me and Gudrun and what had really happened in Iceland, about the Jonsmessa ritual and the shifting back in time, how I knew so much about the real-life Brunhilda. It was a crazy story, I knew, but Anders had pretty much spent his life wrapped up in crazy stories.

"You know, you ought to make your own movies," he said.

"That's what Gudrun thinks too." I laughed.

Gudrun was back at Harvard now, in the musty professorial offices where she'd taken up her role again as the head of Norse mythology and Icelandic saga. We had stayed in touch by email and the other day we Skyped. I'd been excited to tell her about Hammer and Ollie's arrival at my house.

"It's sad that they can never return to Iceland," Gudrun said.

"I know," I agreed, smiling to myself at how I had known she would say that. I wondered if horses could get homesick. I was missing Iceland myself.

"You can always go back," Gudrun told me.

"Yes," I said. "But it wouldn't be the same..."

Without *her*. That was what I wanted to say, but I knew Gudrun understood.

"Are you using my gift?" she asked me. When we'd said goodbye at the airport, she had thrust a package at me and told me not to open it until I was on the plane. I had waited until after take-off to unwrap the paper and inside I had found the familiar burgundy velvet pouch bag that I had seen at Gudrun's side so many times. Gudrun's runes were mine now. I had tried casting them, but I didn't yet have her knack with the symbols.

"All I've predicted so far was a thunderstorm," I said to her. In Otaki there are loads of storms, so I wasn't sure that it was really so clever of me.

There were no signs of rain that evening. The weather was calm and the skies were pink, so I decided to take Hammer on a ride down to the beach. By the time we'd made our way through the bush track to the sand, the sun was low and the water and the sky were both tinged with deep purple. It reminded me of those nights in Iceland when the sun refused to set and I couldn't sleep and the sky would burn and burn forever with this ethereal light.

We rode at a walk along the sand at first, Hammer snorting with excitement when he saw the waves lapping up to him, and then, when the sand was firm enough underfoot, I clucked him forward. As I stayed low in the saddle, he broke into a tölt and we sped across the sands, the sea wind whipping my hair. I was smiling so wide it hurt. I felt like I had never ever been this happy in my whole life and I wondered if I would ever be this happy again.

The beach went on for miles and I could have ridden him like that forever, but eventually the sun began to sink below the horizon and I knew I needed to head home.

I pulled Hammer to a halt and we took one last look out across the sea. The sun was gold on the water and in the dying light Hammer's mane was so brilliant it almost seemed to glow, like there was fire in it. The coarse strands of red and gold seemed to dance like flames before my eyes.

I touched the strands and felt a chill run through me. I looked up at the night sky and suddenly saw a swirl of white. Snowflakes were falling on me. I had to be imagining it – it never snowed in Otaki. But there they were, tiny white flakes whirlpooling around me. I felt their cold kiss on my cheeks and I knew it was real. Hammer's mane was clutched in my hands now, and the strands became flames licking and dancing, drawing me in closer. I closed my eyes and let the fire take me and, when I opened them again, I was no longer on the beach staring out to sea. I was lying in a snowdrift on the banks of a frozen river. Staring down at me, with a staff in his hand and wearing heavy grey robes, was an old man. He was very tall and he had one eye missing. At his feet two enormous grey wolves were flanking him, alert as guard dogs with ears cocked, listening and waiting to see what would happen next.

"All-Father!" I breathed the words.

"*Brunhilda*," Odin replied, "I've been calling you."

CHAPTER 16

Valkyrie

I open my eyes. I'm lying in the snow, staring up at the darkening clouds above me. Already I can see that the ravens are circling over my body, black harbingers of my death.

Am I dead though? My eyes are open and I can see. I try to move my arms and find that my fingers can wriggle and squirm. I'm not in the least cold, despite the snow, which must have been falling on me for a long time because I'm caked in it. My hair, my clothes, even my eyebrows and the tips of my eyelashes are dusted white. I lie still and watch the snow swirling around me and then I hear his voice penetrating the silence.

"Brunhilda!"

He casts a shadow like a mountain as he leans over me.

"All-Father."

"Brunhilda," he says, "I've been calling you."

"I'm sorry," I reply, "I must have been asleep."

I blink away the snow and stare up at him. It's hard not to stare at that black gouged pit where his left eye should be.

He has a staff in his hand made of gnarled wood and he pounds the ground with it now, and the air around us heaves a little, as if the earth is sighing out a breath; and from the grey clouds above, plunging down in a spiral, in a flutter, and with a thrash of wings, two ravens separate from the others and soar to land with claws outstretched, one enormous bird on each of his broad shoulders.

"Hugin and Munin," I say out loud. His ravens, they are, Thought and Memory. Munin, the more inquisitive of the two, turns his head sideways to eye me beadily, and then he pecks a little at Odin's shoulder, and in my mind I can hear the raven as if he's speaking out loud. "Are we sure about her?" Munin says. "She's very young, and very small to be allowed to the great table to feast with the Aesir."

Odin turns his head and looks at Munin, his one eye staring back into the beady eye of the bird. "She is worthy," he growls. "Of all the warriors I have admitted to Valhalla, she is one of the most honourable, and she has shown great valour."

There's a deeper growl than Odin's. A guttural sound, vulpine and dangerous. I look down and see the wolves who flank the All-Father: Geri and Freki, grey and enormous, panting with jaws wide open and eyes glazed.

Odin places a hand down upon Freki's mighty head and the wolf sits down beside him once more, like a well-trained dog. On the other side, Geri whimpers a little and then he drops to his haunches and then down to drape himself faithfully across Odin's feet.

"I have an offer to make you, Brunhilda." Odin's voice is that of a man and yet it rumbles like thunder, shaking the ground and electrifying the air.

"An offer?" I'm anxious. A god has never offered me anything before now – as far as I know.

"Yes," the All-Father says. "I've been watching you. My one eye sees all things, here and now and in the past and the future. I have been greatly impressed by your spirit and your conviction. You are a true Norse warrior. You fought well and died a noble death. You've earned your place at my table. Your mother and father are already there and they wait with the gods to welcome you to our feast."

My parents are waiting for me! And Thor will be there. *Thor!* I can take my seat in the great halls of Valhalla and be greeted as a true warrior...

"Except," Odin says, "...I am wondering, Bru, if you might consider forsaking your seat at the table. I have in mind a greater role for you. I've been thinking of it for some time now."

He smiles at me. At least I think it's a smile. It's hard to tell with a one-eyed god exactly what his face is doing, but I feel the air around me booming like thunder and Hugin and Munin flutter restlessly on his shoulders, so I know that something is definitely up. Odin, the All-Father, is about to make me the offer.

"I have need of a queen. For my Valkyries," he says. "Do you know them?"

Of course I do. They are his angels who search the battlefields and select the warriors who have died valiantly. They lift them up to be admitted to Valhalla.

I don't know what to say. I sit there staring at him, wondering how all of this has happened to me. There was a time when I wanted to be a queen, it's true. But this throne that Odin offers me now is not one I ever thought I would possess.

"It's a great honour," I say. "But I'm not sure that I'm capable of such a thing."

"Oh." Odin looks taken aback. "You'd get wings, of course. Did I mention the wings? You'll find them vital. And there's a lot of singing involved."

I feel my heart beating hard in my chest. "I like to sing," I say.

"Excellent," Odin says. On either side of him the wolves stand to attention. This meeting is clearly coming to its conclusion.

Odin claps his hands together and thunder sounds. Then he spreads his arms wide and reaches out to hug me. I am encircled by the world in his embrace. I can feel the seasons running through my veins, spring and summer, autumn and winter, all melding into one. I feel the grass growing and the tides turning. I'm connected to every living thing and I'm eternal as the dawn. And when Odin steps back from me, I feel this lightness to my being and suddenly I hear a flutter of feathers behind me and I look back and I see that I now have two very large golden wings on my back. All of this is happening very quickly. Too quickly.

"I know," Odin agrees with my thoughts. "It's sudden. I can see that. And perhaps you have something yet to do before you leave this earth and come to join us? Go on. I hear your thoughts and I know you want to see him."

"Would that be all right?" I ask. I don't know the rules about becoming a Valkyrie.

"Of course," the All-Father says kindly. "Go now. I think when you see what he has become, then you will be happy with the choices that you made."

There's the crack of lightning that illuminates the sky above, and the wind swirls the snow so that it blinds me, and when I open my eyes this time, Odin is gone and the ravens and wolves have departed with him. Yet I haven't imagined any of it. I know this because my wings remain. I haven't yet learned to use them, but I experiment a little now. I stretch them out as if I'm splaying out the fingers of my hands, and then I extend them, like I'm stretching my arms wide, and they respond, unfurling, with the feathers dividing and separating and defining themselves ready for flight. And then, very lightly, like a ballerina leaping into the air, I spring off into the sky. My wings catch the wind on an upward gust and they lift me up and very quickly I'm soaring, cresting above the tops of the birch trees and the spruce forests, looking down on the rivers and mountains. The wings give me height and speed and my eyes are as sharp as any eagle's. I'm flying, the wind whipping back my hair, whistling against my golden skin.

Go faster, I think to myself, and my wings adjust their trajectory. Now I'm flying even more swiftly and the fields flash by beneath me and I bank against the wind and turn into it, going inland through the ravines that cut between the mountains, and out the other side where the grass is sweet and the birch trees grow tall.

And then, as the trees clear, on a tussock plateau where the lakes are warm and the skies are blue, I see him.

He is standing with his herd. Over a dozen horses, most of them mares, some of them clearly heavily in foal. He stands proud as he gazes across them. He looks content.

"Jotun!" I call to him, but my voice is lost on the wind. He cannot hear me. I'm on another plane now. We are not together any more. Not as we used to be, when I rode him for miles at a tölt with the wind in my hair and the reins so light in my hands. I will never be with him again in that way, but I have done what

I had to do to make him safe. And that was all I had ever wanted.

"I love you!" I call out again. And even though the wind takes my voice once more, this time he raises his head, and I can see his black eyes beneath that long fringe of fire, and I know that I did what was right. We are both free now.

And in the wind I can hear them singing for me; the other Valkyries are calling me to my new home. It's time to go. I spread my wings so that I hold steady in the wind, gazing over him. It's not for the last time. I will return here. For whenever a warrior has fallen, Odin's call will go out to me. Queen of the Valkyries. And if you are truly brave, I will be there.

Every girl dreams of becoming a princess.
But this real-life princess has a dream of her own.

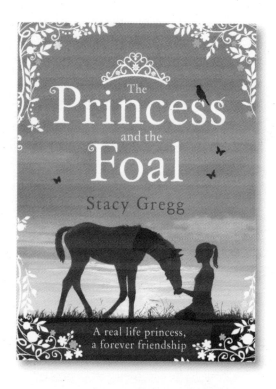

Discover the incredible story
of Princess Haya and her foal.

Two girls divided by time, united by their love
for some very special horses, in this epic
Caribbean adventure.

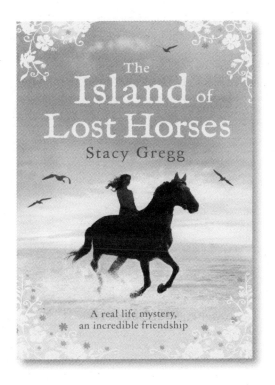

The
Island of
Lost Horses
Stacy Gregg

A real life mystery,
an incredible friendship

Based on the extraordinary true story of the
Abaco Barb, a real-life mystery that has
remained unsolved for over five hundred years.

An epic story of two girls and their bond
with beloved horses, sweeping between Italy
during the Second World War and the present day.

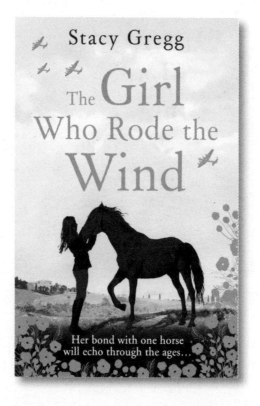

One family's history of adventure and
heartbreak – and how it is tied to the world's
most dangerous horse race, the Palio.

A priceless diamond necklace holds a secret –
the stories of two very different girls…

Anna Orlov lives in a beautiful snowbound palace,
home to a menagerie of wonderful animals – but also
her cruel older brother, Ivan.

Valentina is a circus performer with a very special
horse and big dreams. An epic adventure inspired
by real-life stories.

One girl's refusal to give up, even in the face
of impossible odds...

When an earthquake hits Parnassus on New Zealand's
South Island, Evie and the rest of the town are forced
to evacuate. But when she realises that she'll be forced
to leave her pony, Gus, behind, Evie refuses to join the
others and abandon her best friend...

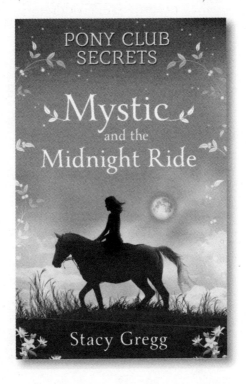

Issie loves horses more than anything!
And she especially loves her pony Mystic at
Chevalier Point Pony Club. So when the unthinkable
happens, Issie is devastated. Then her instructor
asks her to care for Blaze, an abandoned pony,
and Issie's riding skills are really put to the test. Will
she tame the spirited new horse, Blaze? And can
Mystic somehow return to help her...?

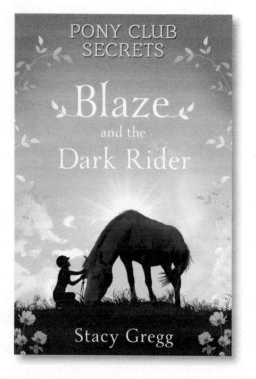

PONY CLUB
SECRETS

Blaze
and the
Dark Rider

Stacy Gregg

Issie is riding for Chevalier Point Pony Club
at the Interclub Shield – the biggest
competition of the year!

But disaster strikes when equipment is
sabotaged and one of the riders is injured.
Issie needs Mystic's help again…

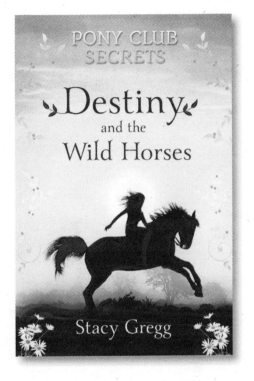

PONY CLUB
SECRETS

Destiny
and the
Wild Horses

Stacy Gregg

Issie and her horse, Blaze, are spending summer
at her aunt's farm instead of at pony club.
When Issie hears of plans to cull a group of
wild ponies she's determined to save them.
This time, Issie is going to need all the
help she can get…

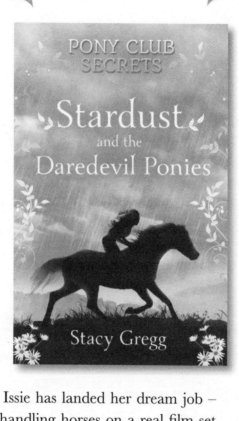

PONY CLUB
SECRETS

Stardust
and the
Daredevil Ponies

Stacy Gregg

Issie has landed her dream job –
handling horses on a real film set.

But what is spoilt star Angelique's big secret?
Could this be Issie's chance for stardom?

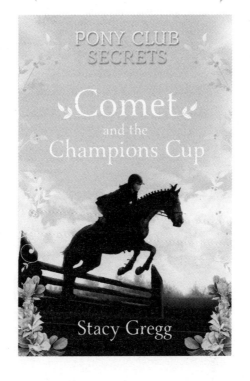

PONY CLUB
SECRETS

Comet
and the
Champions Cup

Stacy Gregg

When Aunty Hess opens a riding school for the
summer, Issie and her friends from pony club jump
at the chance to help. Issie meets the naughty
but talented pony, Comet, who has real
showjumping promise when he isn't misbehaving.
But will she be able to train him in time to compete
at the Horse of the Year show?

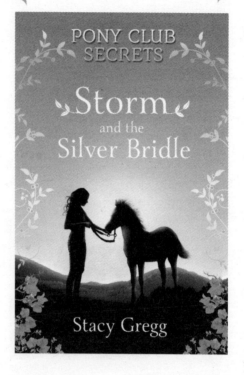

PONY CLUB
SECRETS

Storm
and the
Silver Bridle

Stacy Gregg

Issie's colt, Storm, is growing up fast and attracting
attention at Chevalier Point Pony Club.
Then Storm is stolen – and Issie must travel
to the other side of the world to get him back.
Can she outwit his kidnappers? And is she
brave enough to compete in the ultimate race
for the Silver Bridle?